MAGIC
REPAIR SHOP

Master of Mirrors

Don't miss these other exciting
Magic Repair Shop books!

The Multiplying Menace

The Shape-Shifter's Curse

MAGIC
REPAIR SHOP
Master of Mirrors

Amanda Marrone

Aladdin
New York London Toronto Sydney

ALADDIN

An imprint of Simon & Schuster Children's Publishing Division

1230 Avenue of the Americas, New York, NY 10020

First Aladdin paperback edition March 2011

Copyright © 2011 by Amanda Marrone

All rights reserved, including the right of reproduction in whole or in part in any form.

ALADDIN is a trademark of Simon & Schuster, Inc., and related logo is a registered trademark of Simon & Schuster, Inc.

For information about special discounts for bulk purchases, please contact Simon & Schuster Special Sales at 1-866-506-1949 or business@simonandschuster.com.

The Simon & Schuster Speakers Bureau can bring authors to your live event. For more information or to book an event contact the Simon & Schuster Speakers Bureau at 1-866-248-3049 or visit our website at www.simonspeakers.com.

Designed by Mike Rosamilia

The text of this book was set in Centaur MT.

Manufactured in the United States of America 0211 OFF

2 4 6 8 10 9 7 5 3 1

Library of Congress Control Number 2010931672

ISBN 978-1-4169-9035-2

ISBN 978-1-4391-5824-1 (eBook)

For Helen and Bill Roush, Grandparents Extraordinaire,
whose babysitting duties and support while I wrote
the first book helped make the series possible

Thanks to everyone at Aladdin, especially Fiona Simpson for taking on the third book with magical patience and wisdom. Nothing but good wishes for Patty Schremmer, Scottie Robinson, and Donna Capern, who were in the shop with me at the very beginning, and a cauldron of sparkly spells for Wendy Schmalz and for Kate Angelella, who was dearly missed by Maggie and her friends.

MAGIC
REPAIR SHOP
Master of Mirrors

1

Death Roll

I stood on the banks of the Caledon River, halfway around the world from my new home in Bridgeport, Connecticut. Brown mountains loomed in the distance while bright exotic birds shrieked as they flew by in a burst of color.

I was wearing a purple bathing suit covered with yellow ducks. Oversize flippers clung to my sweating feet, and an orange diving mask was strapped tightly around my head. It would've made for a laughable picture if not for the fact that this was the most important magic repair job I'd ever been asked to do, and if I failed, a young boy would die.

I bit my lip as my stomach flip-flopped like I'd swallowed one of the large fruit bats hanging in the surrounding trees. Yellow crocodile eyes stared at me, unblinking, from the reeds, but these crocodiles weren't who I was looking for. In just a minute I'd use my magically altered reflection to lure a ghost crocodile, Buhodu, from the murky depths of the river, in hopes that he'd take the bait and lead me to his underwater lair.

The only problem was that there was a very good chance I wouldn't make it out of the water alive.

"You *don't* have to do this, Maggie," my friend Raphael said quietly as he stood just behind me on the bank. "No one would blame you if you didn't, and don't forget that a crocodile's bite can inflict five thousand pounds of pressure. Who knows what a *ghost* croc could do?"

"But it's just my reflection he'll be biting down on. It'll be fine," I said, trying to sound braver than I felt. Really, I was scared to death. I'd never used my reflection to tempt anything, let alone a *ghost* crocodile. Things like this just hadn't happened before I'd discovered that I come from a long line of magicians.

Now they happened all too often.

In the past weeks I'd been attacked by a parade of wild animals, and my rabbit, Hasenpfeffer, had almost been killed by a shape-shifter. Not to mention the fact that I was hearing a strange voice coming out of mirrors, and I was sure the crazed magician Milo the Magnificent had something to do with it—even if no one believed me.

I shook my head. Milo was the least of my troubles right now.

The point was, since discovering the magic repair shop, my life had been a series of magical mishaps with no sign of letting up. Just twenty minutes before, Raphael and I had been in the shop grumbling about homework. Before we knew it, we'd been accidentally whisked away through the magic mirror to South Africa, where Mr. McGuire was working on a job. Mr. McGuire had apologized profusely as we'd been dragged out of the crocodile-infested river, but that didn't change the fact that my life was in danger—again.

"I know Mr. McGuire and Mosa will be following you," Raphael continued, "and you'll take that potion to make your reflection taste bad so that spooky croc will spit it out if he tries to eat it, but this is serious business. Business better handled by a grown-up."

I nodded, and turned to see Raphael brushing dark curls off his forehead, his large brown eyes pleading with me to reconsider. When I'd met Raphael three weeks before, he had been green with envy that I had magical powers and he didn't. But now that he knew how dangerous the magic business was, he was constantly suggesting I should retire at the ripe old age of twelve.

I peeked over my shoulder at the small figure of a boy, Aitan. He was sitting as still as a statue with eyes rolled up, unseeing, in his head. He'd been like that since Buhodu had stolen his reflection five days before.

Mosa, the old tribal conjure woman who had summoned Mr. McGuire, now tended the boy—wiping his forehead with a damp cloth and then squeezing drops of water into his mouth. Aitan's mother wept silently at his side, and I knew I would go through with the job even though every fiber of my being was telling me to run.

I jutted my chin out, deciding to at least look like I was feeling brave, and I kept searching the muddied water for any sign of the large ghost crocodile. Mr. McGuire had found a spell that would magically tether someone's reflection to their body, like a hook on a fishing line. He and Mosa weren't powerful enough to pull off the spell, so as much as my legs quivered and my heart raced, it was up to me to help Aitan, or watch him perish.

"How much time will I have to find Aitan's reflection once Buhodu takes the bait?" I asked.

Mr. McGuire walked over to me and scanned the river. "No more than five minutes."

Raphael threw his hands up into the air. "You can't

seriously let Maggie do this! It's crazy!" He gestured wildly at Aitan. "If the tether breaks, she'll be just like him and at the mercy of the live crocodiles in the water—if she doesn't drown first!"

"I'll be following," Mr. McGuire said. He held out the large sea sponge he'd enchanted to act in reverse and allow him to part the water. "You know I'll do everything I can to make sure she's okay."

Mosa rose and stretched her spine straight. "I will go with you too," she declared as she took a twisted stick out of a pocket in the front of her patterned dress. Sparks shot into the air as she held it above her head. "I am deadly accurate with my aim. No crocodile will get close to Maggie!"

"I—I guess we're ready, then," I said.

Mosa scrambled across the sand and searched through a large woven basket sitting next to a makeshift hut that had been erected near the riverbank so she and Aitan's mother could stay close to Aitan. She came up with a jar of red powder and poured some out onto her hand. She smiled and then spit onto the powder and came back to me. "This is a mixture of horseradish root, hot pepper, and magic dust—with a bit of spit to make it stick. Swallow it quickly so it has time to settle. If Buhodu tries to take a bite of your reflection, he will get a hot surprise!"

"After that," Mr. McGuire said, "you can cast the tether spell, and then we'll cross our fingers that Buhodu takes the bait. Let's get started."

A minute later I stared down at my reflection as it rippled in the water. My stomach burned—like an open flame was dancing inside it—from Mosa's peppery mixture.

Mr. McGuire walked a few paces to get a bag from the shade of a tree, and he took out a small vile that shone so brightly, I had to blink and turn away. "This will brighten your reflection to attract the attention of Buhodu," he said, bringing it to me. "I've added some freeze-dried fish heads so you'll be able to hold your breath longer than usual, and otter hair so you can swim swiftly through the water."

I stuck out my tongue. "Fish heads and otter hair? Lovely."

Squinting, I held the golden vial up to my nose and sniffed it. Bile rose in my throat as the rotten fish smell turned my stomach. "Ugh," I muttered, catching a quick glance at what I thought was an actual fish eye in the mixture.

"Hurry," Mosa said. "There is no time to lose."

I plugged my nose, dumped the contents into my mouth, and swallowed it in one gulp. A shiver of disgust ran through me, and then a glowing feeling radiated from my stomach to the tips of my fingers and toes. I felt lighter—almost as though I was about to take off the ground like a balloon. I looked out at my reflection and gasped. It had moved out away from me on the current and was glittering like a sunbeam on the water.

"Quickly!" Mr. McGuire said urgently. "Recite the spell before your reflection floats away!"

I nodded and reached a hand out over the water, my palm facing toward my reflection. *"Reflection of who I really am, go out and travel all the land. Roam the causeways but not too far. Never forget who we are."*

My reflection stopped on the water like someone had anchored it in place. I felt a tugging sensation in my chest as if my reflection was fighting the current to stay close to me, like a kite pulling on a string. I turned to Mr. McGuire. "It worked."

He held out the large sea sponge in one hand and his shiny black wand in the other. "I'm ready if Buhodu should strike."

I looked out over the water. Mosa had told me Buhodu would appear as a ghostly white crocodile, but all of the reptilian shapes I saw now were dark and most definitely living.

Suddenly the crocodiles lurking by the riverbank disappeared from sight one by one with loud splashes and flips of their tails. Fish skipped and danced out across the water, sparkling silver in the sun, to evade some unseen predator.

"He comes," Mosa cried.

A wave of ice-cold terror hit me as my eyes rapidly flicked back and forth on the river, searching for Buhodu. "Where?" Where is he?"

"There!" Raphael called out. "Downriver."

I swallowed hard as an enormous white shape swam smoothly into view. There was no mistaking it for anything but a crocodile, but it glowed in the water like a full moon lighting up the night sky.

"Buhodu," I whispered. I held my breath as he rapidly closed in on my glittering reflection. Mr. McGuire had warned me to brace myself for the bite, and I squeezed my hands into tight fists.

My heart raced as the beast increased his speed, and I screamed when he opened his ghostly jaws and snapped. The tugging sensation in my chest increased as Buhodu turned rapidly, taking my reflection with him. Feeling like an invisible line was pulling me forward, I was yanked off my feet into the river.

I thrashed around for a second or two, the tether to my reflection dragging me through the water. As the bubbles around me cleared, I saw the eerie glow of Buhodu ahead of me in the dim water—my reflection sparkling in his jaws. I pushed my arms through the lily-choked river to follow him, marveling at the ease with which I cut through the water. *Just like an otter,* I thought.

The water around me swirled as though an ocean tide was rushing to the shore, and I saw Mr. McGuire and Mosa. Water sprayed away from them as they held the sea sponges. Mr. McGuire gave me the thumbs up as he and Mosa followed me. I turned and kicked my legs, effortlessly flying through the water after Buhodu. Sparks of blue light cut through the water to my right and left, and I knew Mr. McGuire and Mosa were busy keeping the living, breathing crocodiles away from me.

The creature with my reflection in his jaws slowed, and then dove deeper into a twisted maze of submerged trees. The water was cooler here, and I pulled myself through the branches. Suddenly I saw two brown eyes peering up at me from under a log. I gave a start, and then squinted to make out the figure of a small boy wavering in the water. I'd found Aitan's reflection, but as I swam closer to reach out for it, the great white crocodile turned sharply—swimming between me and the reflection.

The dark eyes set in Buhodu's ghostly white head seemed to bore into me—daring me to steal back what he had taken. My heart raced as my lungs began to burn.

I had to get to Aitan's reflection fast. Buhodu opened his jaws and bellowed, my reflection dangling from his teeth.

You're just a ghost, I said over and over in my head. *Nothing more than a reflection yourself.* With the air in my lungs running out, I headed directly toward the beast. As I swam through Buhodu's ghostly presence and toward Aitan's reflection, an arctic blast shocked my system. I grabbed Aitan's reflection and held it tightly, my lungs desperate for air.

I turned in the water, wondering how I could grab my own reflection, only to see Buhodu snap down on it with five thousand pounds of pressure and start a death roll. I felt the tether snap, and I gasped. I closed my fist tighter around Aitan's reflection as my eyes bulged and my lungs filled with water.

Help me, I thought as the water grew dim. I felt myself sinking to the bottom of the river, soggy branches scratching my skin.

Somebody help me.

2

See No Evil, Hear No Evil, Speak No Evil

I jumped up in bed when my alarm went off the following morning. A fit of coughing wracked me as I leaned over and hit the snooze button. Even though Mosa had cast a healing spell, my lungs still felt waterlogged from the forty seconds I'd been unconscious underwater the day before.

I sighed. Despite everything that had happened, I couldn't keep the corners of my lips from turning up in a smile. Mr. McGuire and Mosa had rescued my reflection after Buhodu had spit it out, and then they'd pulled me from the water—with Aitan's reflection still clutched in my hand.

"Oh," my rabbit, Hasenpfeffer, groaned from his cage. "For pity's sake. Why must I be woken up at this ungodly hour? I don't have a bus to catch or classes to attend. I do need my beauty sleep, though. A rabbit's life span can be greatly shortened by extended periods of disrupted sleep, you know—not to mention poor diet."

I leaned back on my pillows and rolled my eyes. "I don't know of any rabbit who eats as well as you do, *and* you can sleep all you want while I'm at school."

He scoffed. "Not likely. Not with those . . . Never mind." His eyes widened, and then he turned away to drink from his water bottle.

I raised an eyebrow. "Never mind *what?*"

He took a few more licks from his bottle and cleared his throat. "Nothing. I was just talking about the . . . apartment noises. And . . . that . . ." He looked around the room. "That infernal buzzing your computer makes."

"You asked me to leave the computer on so you could surf the Internet while I'm at school."

"Well, yes, but . . . I'll be fine. I'll just go under my blanket; that should muffle the noises."

"You do that."

I shook my head and closed my eyes, and saw Aitan's mother embracing me. I could almost feel her warm tears of happiness against my cheek again.

Aitan would be okay, and Mr. McGuire had banished Buhodu into a holding dimension in the magic mirror. Things were finally looking up.

My breathing relaxed, and I thought I just might be able to catch a few more minutes of sleep.

"Shh."

"I didn't say anything, Hasenpfeffer," I replied.

"I know! I know! Quiet!" a voice that wasn't Hasenpfeffer's snapped.

My eyes flew open, and I froze in place. I'd heard that voice dozens of times in the last few days, and even thought it wasn't Milo's, I couldn't shake the feeling that the evil magician was near.

"I've waited far longer than you," the voice insisted.

"Did—did you hear that, Hasenpfeffer?" I whispered, my own voice shaking. I sat up slowly in my bed, afraid to look up. I swallowed hard, and then tilted my chin up and briefly saw a snatch of red in my mirror.

My heart thumped against my ribs as I jumped to the floor and crouched down by Hasenpfeffer's cage. I stared up at the mirror, but only my window was reflected in it. "Did you see that, Hasenpfeffer? Tell me you saw it! And the voice—you heard that, *right?*"

I looked down, and Hasenpfeffer's head poked out from under his blanket. He yawned dramatically. "What's that? What's all the fuss about? I was just having *the most wonderful* dream about—"

"Come on! You had to have heard it!"

Hasenpfeffer turned his head away from mine. "I didn't hear anything, but frankly, I'd keep this to yourself if I were you. You're grandmother is a bit *concerned* about these *voices* you're hearing."

"I'm a little concerned too!"

"Yes, well, McGuire and that awful Klemp woman have checked out this mirror, and the magic one in the shop as well. And didn't you say they had six different experts examine the not so magical *bathroom* mirror you thought you first heard a voice come from? I know you humans often miss the simplest things, but I have to think that if there was something in those mirrors, surely one of *six* magicians would have found some sort of sign."

"But with Milo trapped in the mirror—"

"The *magic* mirror—in the magic repair shop," Hasenpfeffer said irritably.

"I know which mirror he's trapped in!" I snapped. "But Mr. McGuire told me mirror magic was really complicated, and sometimes portals open up, and maybe . . ."

Hasenpfeffer looked up at me with pity in his pink eyes.

"You really didn't hear anything?" I asked.

"No."

"Maybe I am going crazy. Maybe all the stress—"

"*Sssoon!*" a voice hissed. A peppery smell filled the air, and I saw movement out of the corner of my eye.

My head jerked toward the mirror, and I was sure something white had just darted from view.

"You had to have heard *that!*" I stood up and sniffed the air. It was definitely hot peppers! I stalked toward the mirror. My own tired eyes stared back at me from beneath my messy blond hair. *"Who are you?"* I yelled. *"And why are you doing this to me?* Milo, if you're in there, show yourself!"

Suddenly Gram burst through my door. "Maggie, what's going on? Are you okay?"

Frustrated tears gathered in my eyes. "Gram, I heard the voice again. And I saw that flash of red again too—the exact same shade of red as Milo the Magnificent's cape."

Gram looked down at Hasenpfeffer with wide worried eyes. "Did you hear or see anything?"

Hasenpfeffer shook his head. "I'm afraid not, Gram."

Gram inhaled deeply. "I'm *not* your grandmother!"

Hasenpfeffer turned to me and tilted his head as he looked me up and down. "Tsk. I'm sure it's just that Maggie's overtired, especially after what happened yesterday."

I pointed to the mirror. "The voice came from there; I heard it as clearly as I can hear you. Hasenpfeffer, you had to have heard it. *Please.*"

"Sorry. I didn't hear a thing, but the stress—"

"I'm not stressed!"

Gram's brow furrowed.

"Okay, I'm a little stressed," I admitted wearily.

"Why don't you sit down?" Gram said gently. "You had quite a traumatic experience yesterday." She pursed her lips as she led me back to my bed. "How you keep finding yourself in trouble like this . . . Why, it's just like living with your father all over—"

"What? Like Dad? What do you mean?"

Gram coughed. "Oh," she said, putting a hand to her chest. "It's just that, well, he was always getting into scrapes in the neighborhood. Not like you, of course— no ghost crocodiles and such. Or saving little boys' lives."

She gave me a small smile and patted my hand. When Mr. McGuire had told her what had happened in Africa, she'd yelled so loudly that the Lubchek family in the apartment upstairs had banged on the floor with a broom handle. But once Gram had calmed down, she'd hugged me so tightly it was hard to breath—very unlike Gram—and then she'd told me she was proud and that I was never, ever to do anything like that again.

"I really thought I heard something."

"Why don't you get ready for school," Gram said. "That should take your mind off of things."

My eyes drifted toward my bedroom mirror. "Maybe you're right."

Gram nodded approvingly. "Of course I am. Spending the day with your friends and classmates is just what you need."

When Gram left to get breakfast ready, I quickly got dressed while Hasenpfeffer pretended to snore loudly.

"I know you're awake," I said as I dragged a brush through my hair.

He mumbled as if he was talking in his sleep, and I shook my head. I leaned over, pulled on my sneakers, and then looked out onto the street below. A white cat that had been hanging around stared up at me, and then trotted off between the apartment buildings.

"I think a cat would be a lot easier than a rabbit," I muttered and headed for my door. At the last second I turned back and snatched a small compact mirror off my dresser.

"I know I heard something," I whispered to myself. "And I'm going to prove it."

"Maggie, are you listening?"

I looked up at Raphael and my other best friend, Fiona, watching me from their spot on the rug in our classroom's book nook.

Fiona was twisting one of her long reddish-brown braids. "The numbers *are* pretty shocking," she said.

I looked down at the open compact in my lap and then back up at them again.

"I'm sorry," I said. "I guess I wasn't paying attention."

Raphael held out his hand, and I sighed as I placed the compact into it. "Maggie, this is bordering on obsession," he said.

"If you'd heard it, you'd . . . Never mind. What's this about some numbers?"

He waved a piece of paper filled with mathematical equations at me. "I just spent the last five minutes going over my calculations, and you didn't hear *any* of it?"

I shook my head.

Fiona leaned in close to me. "He's calculated the probability of us dying from some sort of a magical mishap," she whispered. "And the odds are not in our favor."

"The chances of an untimely death resulting from some sort of magical misfire are one in seven," Raphael said solemnly.

I scoffed. "One in seven? Isn't that a little on the high side?" My eyes traced the equations as I tried to make sense of his math. "Well, on the bright side," I said, looking up, "here we all are—alive and well." I gave them a crooked smile. "We just need to keep beating the odds, right? And avoid whatever is stalking me through these mirrors."

Raphael wrinkled his nose and took the paper from me. "Look, it's only a matter of time before you cast some crazy spell or accidentally wish for something and we get eaten by a giant cockroach or sent into outer space, where we agonizingly asphyxiate from the lack of air—if we don't die from an embolism first."

"Okay! Enough! I get it!" I cried.

"Children!" our teacher, Ms. Wiggins, sang out. "The book nook is for losing oneself in the written word, discovering faraway lands, and meeting new friends as they leap off the page into our hearts. It is not for loud voices."

We all nodded, and she stood tall and gave us a salute. For some reason Ms. Wiggins was wearing flowing white pants and a white sailor shirt with a blue bandanna tied around her neck. Her usual wild hair was pulled back into a tight braid, and a round cap sat on her head. We saluted her in return, and she went back to examining a small pirate marionette that Maximilian Litmann was holding up. She took a few steps forward and squinted. "I'm confident we'll figure this out, Max," she declared, taking the puppet from him and making it jump up and down.

Max suddenly stood up, as rigid as a scarecrow, and his fingers began to dance in the air—a sign that he was composing a haiku in his head—one he would no doubt later share with the class, much to Ms. Wiggins's delight.

I turned back to Fiona and Raphael. "I will be extra, extra careful not to make any wishes, especially ones that involve outer space," I said quietly.

"Outer space is a definite no-no," Fiona said, putting a hand to her throat as her eyes bugged out. "At least Mr. McGuire is working on a good-luck potion for you. That'll help improve our chances."

Raphael frowned. "That just goes to show that Mr. McGuire is worried too. This isn't the first time he's tried to magic some extra luck Maggie's way. Face it; bad things happen when you use your magic, Maggie."

"Good things happen too," I insisted. "I saved Aitan and broke a disfiguring hex Milo's duplicate used on Franny. And who knows how many other people would've died if we hadn't stopped Milo's duplicate before he could steal more powers from other magicians."

Fiona shivered and then nibbled on the end of one of her braids. We'd told her about discovering the mummified bodies of several missing magicians in Milo's basement. "And, Raphael, without Maggie's powers we wouldn't have been able to go to Scotland and help the Lachlans," she said, bolstering my defense.

Raphael raised an eyebrow. "Are you forgetting

Hasenpfeffer almost died in Scotland? That *we* could have too? And what about our little trip to Africa, Maggie? You almost didn't come home from that one."

My face clouded over. "But I did. Besides—potion or no potion, I just know my luck is about to change. It has to."

A nervous tickle bubbled up my spine, and I resisted the urge to take back the small mirror from Raphael's hand. All my troubles had started when Milo had come to town. I'd heard the voices again this morning in the girls' bathroom at school. I could have sworn one of the voices was arguing with someone about being "the Master of Mirrors." I didn't bother telling anyone—no one would've believed me anyway—but I knew in my heart that the voice was talking to Milo, and I wasn't done dealing with the evil magician.

Ms. Wiggins clapped her hands. "Children, it's almost time for our assembly. Let's convene on the meeting rug and go over proper assembly behavior."

Serena Gupta started to protest, but Ms. Wiggins held up a hand to silence her. "Given the heckling that caused Magic Manny's tragic unicycle accident, and the jeers that were responsible for the Peaches the Clown's Educational Circus catastrophe, I feel it would be prudent to go over my expectations for your behavior for the show in a"—she held the pirate puppet aloft and grinned crazily—"fun and informative way!"

A collective groan rose around us. I'd been at the Black Rock School for the Gifted and Talented for only a few weeks, but I'd heard enough stories to know that my classmates were a tough crowd and were not above taunting clowns until they cried. Bringing a bunch of know-it-all mature-beyond-their-years sixth graders to a puppet show of *Hansel and Gretel* was just asking for trouble.

We gathered on the rug as Ms. Wiggins fiddled with an old cassette tape player. I settled in between Raphael and Fiona. Max sat with a huge grin on his face, and I knew he was bursting to recite his new poem.

Sal Perez glumly clutched a book on robotics in his lap. "I can't believe we have to give up independent study time to watch a puppet show," he groused.

Nahla Jackson nodded as she absentmindedly played with the beads on pixie braids. "And what educational value is there in sitting through a production of *Hansel and Gretel*? Doesn't Ms. Wiggins know I have to do more research for my science fair project? If I'm going to have any chance of beating Darcy this year, I shouldn't be wasting my time with fairy tales!"

Fiona leaned in close to me. "Is it wrong that I'm actually looking forward to the show?" she whispered.

"No," I whispered back. "I'm looking forward to taking a break from my project on rain forest insects. Did you know that a single square mile of rain forest can have more than fifty thousand insect species in it? That's a ton of insects to research and catalog."

Darcy Davenport led Serena to the rug, and they sat down opposite us.

Fiona smiled at them, but they just stared at us, stone faced. Darcy ran hot and cold—mostly cold—but after she'd helped me out with an extremely difficult spell, I'd thought we'd be able to put our rocky past behind us and maybe even become friends. But after Darcy lost the class election for president to Fiona, she was back to her miserable old self again.

Ms. Wiggins cleared her throat, and I looked up to see her standing over us with the puppet dangling from one hand. She flicked her wrist, and the puppet's wooden head bobbed up and down on its string. She pushed play on her tape recorder, and the air was filled with the sound of crashing waves and gull cries.

"Ahoy!" she said in a high-pitched voice from the corner her mouth. "My name is Captain Manners, and I'll be talking to you about today's exciting assembly!"

3
The Show Must Go On

"Ahoy, Captain Manners!" Max said, giving the puppet a hearty salute.

Darcy rolled her eyes. *"Captain Manners?"* she muttered under her breath. "Oh, please."

Serena sniggered, and Nahla covered her mouth with her hands to keep from laughing. I felt bad for Ms. Wiggins, but between the sailor suit and the puppet, I was having trouble keeping a straight face myself. Only Max was gazing happily at Captain Manners.

Darcy sat up straight, smoothed down her frizzy hair, and then raised her hand.

"Yes, Darcy?" Ms. Wiggins said in the puppet's voice.

Darcy scowled at the puppet. "Does my mother know about this assembly? Because I think she'd be extremely unhappy to have us wasting class time to see a puppet show better suited for kindergartners. And after we spent countless hours last week creating Asian textile weavings, I really think we should be concentrating on our academics. I have college to think about, and hand-spun yarn and marionettes are not going to get me into Harvard!"

Ms. Wiggins lowered Captain Manners and shook her head sadly—her eyes welling up with tears. "You're only twelve years old, yet you're ready to throw away the magic of childhood just to get into a good college. My heart— and that of Captain Manners—weeps for you."

Darcy's mouth dropped open in protest, but before she could speak, Ms. Wiggins dangled the puppet in front of her. "And this attitude," she said in the squeaky voice, "is precisely why it is so important that you take leave of your studies and enjoy the magic of puppetry, if only for an afternoon."

Ms. Wiggins had Captain Manners do a jaunty dance, and then the puppet bowed in front of Darcy and Serena.

Despite their horrified looks, Ms. Wiggins continued in her own soothing voice. "This may come as a surprise, Darcy, but it was actually your mother who booked the

Webb Family's Stringless Marionettes to perform at the school today. And I'll let you in on a little secret. After I decided to dedicate my life to enriching the minds of young children, I put myself through a non–Ivy League college by performing puppet shows at day cares and street festivals. I was Sailor Wiggins, first mate to Captain Manners, the pirate of good behavior."

She tilted her hand so the sword-wielding arm raised high in the air, and using Captain Manners's voice, she began to lecture us about what comments were and were not appropriate when viewing a performance.

Five minutes later Captain Manners took his final bow and Ms. Wiggins gulped some water to soothe her strained vocal cords. "Now, children, I hope you will take Captain Manners's lesson to heart, and we can all enjoy the assembly without worrying about the performers suing the school for physical or emotional damage."

We all nodded, and Ms. Wiggins clutched her chest. "I know you children will do the right thing, but before we leave for the assembly, Max would like to grace us with his latest haiku." She nodded to Max. "Why don't you stand up and take Captain Manners to enhance your presentation. It will give us a chance to practice being respectful audience members."

Max eagerly took Captain Manners and tilted the

wooden handpiece awkwardly. "Since the Webb family marionettes are supposed to be 'stringless,' Ms. Wiggins and I were experimenting with different kinds of string to see which ones would be difficult for an audience to see." His eyes widened. "Suddenly inspiration struck."

Darcy groaned. Ms. Wiggins glared at her and then smiled at Max. "Go on, dear," she said. "Hold your chin up high and recite your haiku with pride!"

Max raised his chin and moved the Captain Manners controller, making the puppet awkwardly flail its limbs. "Ride the wind-tossed waves, a pirate scans the horizon, dolphins at his side."

Darcy sneered. "'A pirate scans the horizon' has eight syllables."

Max's round cheeks reddened as Captain Manners fell from his hand. He moved his fingers as he mouthed the words to his haiku. "Eight!" he whispered in horror. "How could I have done that?"

"That's all right, Max," Ms. Wiggins cooed as she picked the puppet up. "It was a simple mistake."

"No wonder his publisher turned down his latest book," Darcy muttered a little too loudly.

Fiona jumped up and patted Max on the shoulder. "Don't worry about it, Max." She gave Darcy the evil eye. "Writing is all about revising. Ms. Wiggins tells us that all the time. I like that you're not afraid to show us the real you."

I nodded in agreement. "And it's nice you have a creative side—something that is seriously lacking in this room."

"And sometimes your haikus make me laugh," Nahla added. "Even if they're not supposed to."

Ms. Wiggins let out a tremendous sob of happiness. "See people? This is what I'm talking about. This is what is truly important. Embracing our differences in a judgment-free environment trumps getting into an Ivy League school any day." She gasped, bringing a fluttering hand to her mouth. "Children, I have just had the most *brilliant* idea!" She flung her arms over her head to emphasize the words.

"In order to help you embrace your differences, you'll work in pairs to create a puppet show that highlights your unique talents in a collaborative way. You can make marionettes, or even sock puppets—anything you wish. The point is to really get to know one of your classmates and celebrate his or her unique talents. I want you to really see what makes each and every one of you a *blossoming star*."

Darcy's mouth dropped open. "Wait! My schedule is completely booked. I don't have time—," she began, but Ms. Wiggins bugged her eyes out and held her hand out like a policeman stopping traffic.

"Not another word, Ms. Davenport!" she said sternly. Ms. Wiggins sniffed and regarded us. "Now let's see. Nahla, I think you and Sal should work together. Raphael and . . . Fiona. Max and . . ."

Max's lower lip trembled. "Not Darcy. Not Darcy. Not Darcy," he whispered.

"Serena!" Ms. Wiggins said. "That leaves Maggie and Darcy as our final pair."

My heart sank as Ms. Wiggins nodded her head. "Yes," she said. "I think these groupings will work out perfectly! Now let's soak in some inspiration watching the Webb Family's Stringless Marionettes performance of *Hansel and Gretel!*"

Darcy looked at me; her lip curled in disgust.

I wrinkled my nose. "I can't wait to work with you, either," I said in a hushed voice.

Ms. Wiggins waved us to the door. "Let's be the best possible audience we can be, boys and girls," she squeaked. "And I'm sure the show will go off without a hitch."

As we gathered in the auditorium, Darcy's mother rushed over to us. She was dressed in a pale blue pantsuit, and her short blond hair was sprayed into a stiff bob. "Here you are. I was getting worried you were going to be late. Since I arranged this assembly, I was able to convince Headmaster Petrie to allow the sixth graders to have the front row, so follow me."

She stopped and raised an eyebrow at Ms. Wiggins. "Alberta, what an interesting choice of outfit you have on today. Going to swab the poop deck, are we?"

Ms. Wiggins blushed as she looked down at her sailor suit. "Oh no! I was simply embracing the spirit of today's assembly. I was once a practicing puppet artist. I went by the name Sailor Wiggins, and I entertained children with a marionette I hand-carved from a renewable wood source. I even sewed his little pirate suit myself. Would you like me to go back to the classroom and get Captain Manners?"

Mrs. Davenport's smile froze on her face for a second. "Hand-carved, you say? My. My, you are just full of surprises, Alberta, but the show is about to begin. I will make sure to have Darcy tell us all about Captain Manners at dinner tonight, though."

She paused and looked Ms. Wiggins up and down. "Perhaps you might consider a career with your little puppet someday soon?"

Ms. Wiggins shook her head. "Oh, I couldn't bear to leave the children. I have so many life lessons to teach them. They are woefully unschooled in the more mystical aspects of the universe that can bring balance and harmony to oneself."

Mrs. Davenport nodded. "Hmm. Lucky us that you're so dedicated, eh? Well, why don't you all take your seats, and I'll begin the program."

As we filed into our row, Darcy pulled her mother aside. "Puppets, Mother?" Darcy said in a hushed voice. "Really? You know I have a ton of work to do. Nahla is breathing down my neck trying to win the science fair this year."

"Keep your voice down, Darcy," Mrs. Davenport said through clenched teeth. "I had to bring them in as a favor, but it should be a marked improvement from the last magical act we had here."

Mrs. Davenport looked my way with narrowed eyes like it was my fault her cousin Milo had been trapped in the magic mirror on this very stage. I turned away and sighed.

"Just ignore her," Raphael whispered. "We both know Milo got himself stuck in the mirror."

"Yes, but Mrs. Davenport still blames me."

The lights dimmed, and Darcy pushed her way past us to sit in the seat Serena had saved for her. "Hope they don't ask for volunteers," she hissed as she went by. "We all know how you two messed up the last show."

Raphael and I exchanged exasperated looks. We had been forced to "volunteer" at Milo's show, and it had almost gotten us killed.

Mrs. Davenport walked up the steps leading to the stage and then crossed to the center. She turned on a microphone, tapped it to see if it was on, and then smiled broadly. "Hello, everyone. It gives me great pleasure to welcome the Webb Family's Stringless Marionettes to the Black Rock School for the Gifted and Talented. I had the privilege of seeing a bit of the rehearsal, and I know you'll be as astounded as I was when I saw the puppets in action. Mr. Webb has asked me to remind you that there is no talking or cell phone use during the performance, as it's distracting to the puppets."

The audience tittered.

Mrs. Davenport's eyes widened, and she quickly leaned in closer to the microphone. "I, er, mean, it's distracting to the *puppeteers!*" She waved her hands toward us. "Anyway, you are in for a fabulous show, and I dare you to try to figure out how they make those little puppets sing and dance with no strings! So let's give a Black Rock round of applause for today's production of *Hansel and Gretel!*"

Ms. Wiggins applauded wildly. "I cannot *wait* to see this!"

As Mrs. Davenport exited to the audience, the curtain parted to the sounds of soft orchestrations. A woodland scene was on the stage, with a rickety cottage painted on the backdrop.

A small girl puppet, obviously Gretel, skipped out onto the stage with a basket hanging from the crook of one of her wooden arms. The music swelled, and the puppet looked into her basket and then out over us with large painted blue eyes. She blinked wooden eyelids with an audible clack and started to sing about how hungry she was and how she'd been unable to find even a crumb of food in the forest.

Murmurs rose up from the audience. Necks craned toward the stage, and eyes squinted as everyone tried to figure out how the little puppet was moving across the stage, seemingly on its own.

Fiona and Raphael elbowed me gently from either side. "Magic?" they whispered in unison.

I looked back up at Gretel's jointed mouth moving as she trilled her song. It was obvious the voice was coming right out of the puppet and not from someone behind the scenes. "Mrs. Davenport said this would be an improvement over the *last magical* act," I whispered back. "Which implies this one is magic too."

Raphael sighed. "This is going to end badly, isn't it?"

I shook my head. "What could go wrong with a puppet show?"

As Gretel's song ended, the Hansel puppet danced out wearing a pair of shorts held up with flowered suspenders.

"Oh, Gretel," Hansel said in a high-pitched voice. "I too have found no food in the forest. Our stepmother will be so very upset. Whatever shall we do?" he asked stiffly.

Darcy sniggered. "I guess they thought going string-less was supposed to make up for the *bad* acting."

The Hansel puppet zeroed in on Darcy, and his blue eyes seemed to darken.

Gretel cleared her throat. "*Hansel,*" she implored, "per-haps we can find some mushrooms here by the edge of the house." She waited for a few seconds, but Hansel didn't respond. "*Brother dear,* shall we hunt for *mushrooms?*"

Hansel gave Darcy one last glare, clicked his eyelids, and then skipped toward his sister. "Yes, Gretel, mush-rooms would make our stepmother very happy, for she could cook them in a soup and fill our empty tummies."

As the two puppets bent over, a spotlight illuminated the cottage, and the shadowed outlines of a man and woman appeared inside.

"We don't have enough food to feed the four of us," the woman began. "We must take the children into the woods and leave them, or else we will starve!"

"We cannot abandon the children," the man said. "Oh, we cannot. I would rather perish."

The woman's shadowy arms swung out. "Then we will all *die!*"

The man hung his head. "Very well. I'll do it."

The spotlight went out, and another light hit Hansel and Gretel. "Oh my," Gretel said, bringing her wooden hand to her mouth. "Did you hear that? We shall *surely* perish."

"I'm about to perish from boredom," Darcy said.

Shushes rose up around her, and as much as I hated to admit it, I felt the same way. The show was terrible. I looked back up to see Hansel glaring at Darcy again.

"*Hansel?*" Gretel said urgently as her jointed fingers tapped her brother's shoulders. "Did you hear me? *We shall surely perish*. But perhaps *you* can think of a way to save us?"

Hansel turned to Gretel and nodded his wooden head. "Fear not, dear Sister. We shall gather white stones and drop them as we go into the forest. The full moon will illuminate them and we will find our way home and *not* perish."

"Yes, yes. Let us fill our pockets with stones!" Gretel agreed.

They began to sing about their plan as they gathered the small white rocks from the stage. Darcy groaned, making no effort to hide her disdain for the production. "Perhaps they can find a better lyricist in the forest. This stuff is worse than Max's haikus."

Serena laughed. "I think they've got rocks in their little wooden heads."

"Girls!" Ms. Wiggins admonished from several seats away. "Remember what Captain Manners told you," she whispered.

"But, Ms. Wiggins," Darcy whispered loudly, "this is awful!"

Ms. Wiggins grimaced, and it was obvious she was finding the show as painful to watch as everyone else.

Gretel turned her head sharply toward Darcy and Serena. Her blue eyes darkened like Hansel's had before. *"That's it!"* she spit.

Hansel smiled maniacally. "Are you thinking what I'm thinking, *Sister*?"

Gretel's head bobbled up and down. "Yes, *dear Brother*, I think I am."

4

Thanks for the Memories

Hansel and Gretel flew across the stage, rapidly stuffing their pockets with rocks. The audience laughed as the puppets sang their song at high speed, completely out of sync with the music.

Worried voices could be heard from backstage. "Puppets, please, stay on script," someone called out. "Please!"

Hansel laughed. "We're improvising!"

When all the stones had been gathered, the brother and sister puppets walked to the edge of the stage. "Ladies and Gentleman," Gretel began.

"And rude little girls," Hansel continued. "We've decided to rewrite the script."

"Puppets, no!" someone called out from the wings.

Hansel and Gretel reached into their pockets and each pulled out a round white stone. "Rocks in our heads?" they said in unison. "How about rocks in the audience?"

"I knew it," Raphael said as he ducked down in his seat.

Instantly the duo started throwing the stones toward us all with rapid speed.

"Let's go backstage and see if we can help!" I cried. Fiona and Raphael nodded, and we linked hands and pushed through the children rushing from the auditorium to a cacophony of teachers yelling for order and squeals as rocks connected with bodies and heads.

Hansel and Gretel's triumphant cries echoed around us, and we raced up the stairs to the stage. "Close the curtains," I yelled to Raphael.

The puppets turned to us and started volleying rocks our way. "Hey, quit it!" I cried. "I'm trying to help!"

Hansel laughed. "Close range—easy pickings," he said gleefully, throwing another rock and hitting me in the shoulder.

"Ow!"

"Maggie, I think the last thing they want is someone

shouting orders at them," Fiona said as Raphael finished closing the curtains. "They need our understanding."

Hansel and Gretel stopped and regarded her.

Fiona clasped her hands and looked sympathetically at the two. "I'm sorry my classmates were so rude; the show was really good."

Hansel blew a noisy raspberry. "The show's a huge stink bomb, and you know it!" He threw a stone at her, and she jumped aside to avoid it.

"Hey!" Fiona cried. "I was trying to be nice!"

A man with wild white hair and a long handlebar mustache hustled onto the stage. "Puppets!" He said angrily. "Stop it this instant!"

He gasped when he saw Raphael, Fiona, and me. "Oh, I didn't know there were children here." He gulped. "I guess you know my secret now. My little puppets are . . . robots! Yes, *robots*." He gave us a strained smile. "Please don't tell anyone about my little robot puppets. I don't want to spoil the illusion."

I shook my head. "It's okay. We know you're using magic, but we won't tell anyone."

The man brought his hand to his chest. "You know?"

"Maggie is a magician too," Raphael said, pointing to me.

The man let out a long sigh. "I am Mr. Webb, and

I apologize for my puppets." He shook a fist angrily at them. "It would serve you right if I kept you all like this!"

Hansel and Gretel rushed over to Mr. Webb. "We're sorry," they cried.

Gretel wrung her hands. "It won't happen again. We swear!"

A large witch marionette clopped in from the left wing of the stage, followed by the stepmother and father. The witch's wooden fingers gripped a gnarled walking stick, which she pointed at Mr. Webb. "We had nothing to do with this debacle!" she cried. "We were waiting patiently for our cues. We should not be punished."

Hansel rolled his painted eyes. "Please. You went totally off script last week, and it took the two of us to push you into the oven during yesterday's performance!"

"And you two," Gretel said, pointing at the parents, "refused to sing the song in act two last week."

"But the words are embarrassing!" the stepmother marionette exclaimed.

"And you're always banging my head on the oven when you push me in," the witch fired back.

Suddenly Mrs. Davenport pushed through the curtains. "Well, this is a fine mess! Mr. Webb, I agreed to hire you as a favor to my mother-in-law, and this is what I get—mayhem and . . ." She paused when she saw us. Her mouth formed and angry pucker. "Oh, why am I not surprised to see you three here?"

"We just came back to see if we could help," I said.

Mr. Webb hung his head. "I'm so sorry, Delilah. There was a child heckling the puppets from the first row. They don't like performing as it is, but to be taunted from the audience—well, it was too much."

Raphael folded his arms across his chest. "It was Darcy."

Mrs. Davenport's cheeks reddened, but she held her head high. "Well, these things happen. But you certainly can't blame a small child for what went on. I mean, really! Tossing rocks? What's next, chucking audience members into the witch's oven?"

"I'm sorry," Mr. Webb said again.

She sniffed. "Well, we'll have to find someone to cast a memory damper before the day is out so this unfortunate incident will be forgotten by everyone. My reputation is on the line, and the last thing I need is for angry parents to call in about a show sponsored by me!"

Mr. Webb whistled. "Cast a memory damper on the whole school? You'd have to be pretty powerful to pull off a spell like that."

"I'll bet Maggie can do it," Fiona said. "She's a level one hundred!"

"Oh!" declared Mr. Webb. "So young, and with so much power."

Mrs. Davenport's eyes bugged. "*Level one hundred?* I must say, you have quite an imagination, Ms. Fitzgerald!"

"No," Raphael said. "Sir Lachlan sent Maggie's World Federation of Magic license last week. I've seen it myself. She's a level one hundred."

Mrs. Davenport stared at me. "*You?* Level one hundred?"

"Yes," I said quietly. I didn't bother to tell her that Sir Lachlan thought my powers were likely much higher. He thought that sort of information was best kept quiet.

Mrs. Davenport smiled stiffly. "Well, isn't that *nice* for you. I guess you're the perfect person to cast the spell. I'll contact Mr. McGuire and see if he can get to the school with the supplies we need. I'll tell your teacher you're helping Mr. Webb pack up. And you . . ." She turned to Mr. Webb. "I suggest you figure out how to get these *puppets* to start following orders. Otherwise you'll need to be casting memory spells at all your shows!"

She took out a cell phone and headed backstage.

Mr. Webb scowled at his marionettes and then took out a wand covered in faded black paint. "All of you, come!"

The stepmother, father, and witch marionettes joined

Hansel and Gretel, and Mr. Webb pointed his wand at them. *"The show is over, curtains closed. Return to normal, the ruse exposed."*

A foggy mist shot out of the tip of the wand and surrounded the group. The puppets seemed to blur in the haze—their faces dripping like melting wax. As the mist cleared, five small creatures stood in their places. Their skin was brown and leathered with age, and two pointed ears poked through the messy brown hair on each of their heads. They were dressed in an assortment of brown hand-stitched clothing.

"They're elves!" Fiona cried.

Mr. Webb shook his head. "No. House brownies. *Ungrateful* house brownies!

The brownies held their hands out and stretched their limbs, obviously happy to be free from the spell that had transformed them into wooden puppets.

"Now go and get in the travel box before anyone else sees you!" Mr. Webb commanded. "And no nonsense or I'll turn you back into marionettes."

The brownies scowled, and muttered bitterly, but they hustled quickly offstage.

Mr. Webb shook his head. "They've been with my family for more than a hundred years. Brownies like to help around the house—washing dishes and such in exchange for bowls of milk and other simple fair. Unfortunately, with all of our modern appliances, there wasn't much for them to do, and with the arthritis in my fingers, working my marionettes was getting difficult. I'd thought I could solve two problems at once by having the brownies work in the show."

He looked into the wing. "Sadly, they've never been happy performing."

"Couldn't you just let them do the dishes?" Fiona asked.

"They know it would be me taking pity on them, as I could easily pop the plates and glasses into the dishwasher. They're only happy if they truly feel needed." He sighed. "I thought this was the way."

His shoulders slumped, and he regarded the stage. "Perhaps you could help me with the sets while we wait for Mr. McGuire?" His lips turned up into a weary smile. "It's been ages since I've seen him. He was the one who helped me come up with the spell to transform the brownies. I still remember the day he opened the repair shop with Jerry Malloy. Now, that was a magician to be reckoned with!"

"Jerry Malloy was my grandfather," I said.

Mr. Webb looked me up and down. "That explains where you got your level one hundred from. Your grandfather was famous for being an overachiever. He tried to keep it quiet, but word gets out about things like that.

"Funny thing, I remember being in the shop many years ago to get some supplies, and your grandfather was researching a memory damper spell. He was in a foul mood at the time—never did say whose memory needed a bit of altering, but it seems things have come full circle. I guess it runs in the family."

Half an hour later all the backdrops and props were packed away and Mrs. Davenport returned with Mr. McGuire. "Against my better judgment," she said, coming in from stage left, "my mother-in-law persuaded me to have Mr. Webb come to the school. Seems he's been having trouble booking gigs. Of course, now I know why."

I cleared my throat, and Mrs. Davenport looked up to see Mr. Webb frowning at her. "Oh, don't look at me like that. Your show was a complete disaster and a public relations nightmare for me. But I'm sure once you get those little brownies in line—and perhaps get them some acting and singing lessons—you'll have no trouble booking jobs!" she said cheerily.

"Good to see you, Hans," Mr. McGuire said, extending a hand to Mr. Webb.

"Gregory!" Mr. Webb exclaimed, shaking his hand warmly. "What happened to your hair, and why didn't you magic it back into place?"

"Hans, do you know how expensive hair regrowth potions are?"

Mr. Webb ran his fingers through his wild white hair. "Actually, I do."

"Gentleman," Mrs. Davenport said, "the school day is almost over, and we need to get that memory damper going soon. You can talk about your hair"—she regarded Mr. McGuire with a smirk—"or lack thereof, afterward."

Mr. McGuire placed a tote bag on the stage. He looked around and clucked his tongue sadly. "Hard to believe we were on this very spot not too long ago. Hopefully, this repair job will have a better outcome. The spell is simple enough to execute. You need to be a level ninety to pull it off." He smiled. "Luckily, that won't be a problem for you, Maggie."

Mrs. Davenport rolled her eyes.

"Delilah, you need to decide if you want to remember the show or not," Mr. McGuire said.

She fluffed her hair with her hands. "Better to remember the whole unfortunate event than suffer the consequences in case she botches the spell."

"Very well. You'll have to stand behind Maggie, then, to avoid the bubbles."

"Bubbles?" Fiona asked.

"Yes. Maggie will dispense the spell with a bubble wand. It's the best way to disperse a spell over a wide area."

Raphael raised his eyebrows. "What if the bubbles get out a window and land on some passerby? Will it affect their memory?"

"No," Mr. McGuire said. "The spell I've come up with is specific to the show. Mrs. Davenport told me about the rocks, so I configured the potion so that anytime someone thinks about the show and the rocks, they'll have trouble fully remembering it. I also added bits of what they should have seen had the show gone without a hitch."

"Amazing!" Fiona exclaimed.

Mrs. Davenport shook her head. "Non-magical people are so easily amused. I suppose I should do a room check and make sure each classroom door is open."

Mr. McGuire nodded. "Good thinking. We'll wait for your return before we send the spell off. Raphael," Mr. McGuire continued, "can you look at the square footage of the school I have on this piece of paper and look at the dispersal speed and see if you can calculate how long Maggie needs to keep at it before the bubbles will have reached every classroom?"

"I'm on it," he said, taking the paper from Mr. McGuire.

"Great. Now all we need to do is mix the ingredients." He took out a tall, skinny plastic container filled with what looked like churning smoke, and another bubbling with an iridescent color.

"What's in them?" I asked.

He held out the dark container. "In this one I've added smog and a little bit of magic to make the memory hazy. In this other I have a dime-store bubble mixture—with a few extra ingredients. I typed up what I wanted everyone to forget, and what to remember in its place, and then pulverized the paper in a food processor with rainbow water. The rainbow water will give the bubbles an attractive sheen so people will be compelled to touch them. Once the bubbles pop, the smog will blur the bad memory, and magic dust number seven will make sure the new memories stick."

He took a long bubble wand out of his bag. "You'll need this as well." He then opened the container of rainbow water, and the scent of a fresh spring rain filled the air. "Okay, here's the spell," he said, handing me a piece of paper. "I'll combine the bubble mixture and the smog, and then you recite the spell and start blowing. Oh, I almost forgot!"

He took out another, smaller container that had a

swirling vortex swishing around noisily inside. "You'll need to inhale this. It will help the bubbles reach their destination faster." He held out the jar, and as I took a step closer to examine it, the hissing of the viscous winds inside made goose bumps crop up on my arms.

"It's just a small piece of a tornado. Like I said, it'll get the bubbles moving faster."

I grimaced. *"Tornado?"*

He smiled at me. "I hear it smells like cotton candy," he said with a wink.

"Yeah, right." I looked down at the spell and then back at the jar. "I guess we should get going. Raphael, could you open the curtains again so the bubbles can get out easier."

He looked up from his calculations. "Will do Captain Bubbles." He saluted me and laughed.

"Ha, ha."

"Based on my figures," he said, standing up, "with the wind speed generated by the tornado-strength winds, you'll need to blow bubbles for only five minutes."

"I'll prop open the doors to the auditorium," Fiona cried.

Mrs. Davenport entered as Fiona opened the first door. "All the rooms are ready."

Mr. McGuire nodded and then mixed the two containers together. "Everyone, get behind Maggie."

Fiona, Raphael, Mr. Webb, and Mrs. Davenport scurried into place.

"Now recite the spell," he said, handing me the mixture. "Then breathe in the tornado and blow out some bubbles!"

I swallowed hard and took a deep breath. *"The show is over, now time to review. Demand a rewrite; rework it through. As we send the new ending up into the air, memories will fade to avoid all despair."*

After I recited the spell, Mr. McGuire quickly unscrewed the lid on the jar and stuck it under my nose. I inhaled deeply and almost choked as the wind raced up my nose and filled my lungs almost to bursting.

"It does not smell like cotton candy!" I said, coughing. "More like dust."

I took the bubble wand and dipped it into the mixture. When I pulled it out, it was coated in a sticky film that glistened like a rainbow as it stretched across the wand's loop. I blew gently like I would've if I'd simply been blowing bubbles on a hot summer's day, but my breath flew out of me like a raging wind. Thousands of bubbles flooded into the air and were carried away through the auditorium doors.

Raphael kept time, and when five minutes had passed, I put the wand back into the container for good.

"Do you think it worked?" I asked.

Just then Ms. Wiggins came in. "Children!" she called out. "You need to come back to class so we can finalize details for your puppetry project. Oh, and Mr. Webb— bravo! I am still completely baffled by how you got your marionettes to appear like they were walking and talking on their own. Why, they almost seemed like living and breathing creatures."

She sniffed and dabbed her eyes. "I'm getting choked up just thinking about dear, sweet Hansel and Gretel reuniting with their father. And when they revealed that their pockets were lined with jewels, ensuring they'd never go hungry again—well, *bravo*," she sobbed. "I just wish I knew why I have this bruise on my forehead. It's almost like I bumped my head on something."

"Something like a rock," Raphael said quietly.

"It worked," Fiona whispered.

I sighed. "At least that problem is fixed. Now on to the next one. Working with Darcy on this project is sure to be a disaster."

5

Kobold Blues

After school I raced into my bedroom.

"Thank goodness you're home!" Hasenpfeffer squealed as he poked his head from under the blanket in his cage. He raced out and ran in circles around me. "Oh, I've had the most horrific day! I had to keep pinching myself to make sure I wasn't dreaming, although I wished I was, because then I could wake up and everything would be back to normal. And it's not easy pinching yourself without opposable thumbs!"

I flung my backpack onto the floor by my closet. "I'll bet you a million bucks my day was worse. I was attacked by rock-wielding puppets, had to swallow a tornado, and—even worse—Darcy and I got assigned to work together on a project. She insisted we get started right away, even though it makes more sense to do it tomorrow, when we don't have school. But she'll be here any minute, and my room is a mess, the breakfast dishes are still in the sink, and there's a coating of dust over all the furniture."

My eyes traced my unmade bed and my dirty clothes on the floor. It was tempting to make a wish to clean it up, but despite being at least a level one hundred magician, wish magic often backfired, and the last thing I wanted was to have all my underwear flying out of the dresser just as Darcy arrived.

"I guess I'm a millionaire, then," Hasenpfeffer declared. "My day went downhill right after you left for school. First I—"

"I really don't have time for another rant about how your parsley wasn't fresh, or it was the wrong kind, or your blanket isn't soft enough, or there was a draft and you almost caught pneumonia." I pulled my comforter up and straightened my pillow, thinking Hasenpfeffer's near-death experience hadn't sweetened his personality any. If anything, it had just made him more demanding, as he was determined to live "every moment to its fullest."

Hasenpfeffer sat up on his haunches. "Maggie! You

need to listen to me before something bad happens! There's this white cat that keeps appearing, and—"

"Later," I insisted. "Darcy will be here any second. "Close your eyes while I change out of my uniform."

I pulled off my uniform and threw on a T-shirt and jeans. Then I rushed out to the kitchen to clear the sink, with Hasenpfeffer scampering behind me. "Maggie! I really need to tell you—"

"I'll get you some parsley as soon as I get these plates into the dishwasher."

Hasenpfeffer sighed. "Fine. If that's the way you want it. But don't blame me when the trouble starts. I think I'll just hide under the couch and pretend I'm not here."

"That's a great idea. That way you won't have to talk to Darcy."

He sniffed indignantly. "It's not Darcy I'm worried about. It's that creature in the mirror who's been muttering on and on for the past week."

I froze as an icy chill ran up my spine. "What?" I turned toward him, my heart pounding in my chest. "Did you say 'creature in the mirror'? You heard it too, didn't you?"

"Yes, but never mind all that. You keep tidying up. That's more important. I probably shouldn't even mention the ghost." He hopped toward the couch and started to wiggle himself under it. "Why, I'd bet a million dollars that its *dire* warning is all a bunch of nonsense."

"Ghost? Warning? Hasenpfeffer, what are you talking about?" I ran over and pulled him out before he could disappear under the couch.

He sat up and gave his ears a good long scratch, and then smoothed the fur on his legs. "Are you sure the dishes can wait?"

"Yeeees!" I said slowly. "Now talk! Starting with why you didn't tell me you could hear the voice coming out of the mirror? I only asked you a dozen times!"

Hasenpfeffer looked away. "At first I thought that I might have been hallucinating—you know, some kind of after-effect from the bite I got from that shape-shifter—or that your craziness was contagious. You never know with you magic people, but I saw how everyone treated you—like you were mad. I had no doubt your grandmother would turn me out on the street if she thought I was encouraging you."

The doorbell rang, and I groaned. "Oh, great. Darcy!" I buried my head in my hands. "Let me get rid of her, and then you can tell me what happened."

I took a deep breath and opened the door. Darcy was standing there still wearing her school uniform, with a huge tote bag overflowing with fabric and string. She pushed me aside and barged in without even saying hello.

"I have a bunch of supplies we can use, but we can magic anything else we might need—the *one* good thing about doing this project with you—but you need to get something straight. This may be a totally lame project, but I still want ours to be the best. I just know Max is cooking up something sappy that Ms. Wiggins will inexplicably think is brilliant; so I am not above doing something over-the-top sentimental. I've made a list of my talents, and you can help me narrow them down because the presentation has to be less than five minutes."

She put her bag on the floor and looked around the apartment. "This is cozy."

"Look, Darcy—"

"Oh! Did I mention I brought string? But on the way over, I got to thinking we may want to do shadow puppets." She continued ignoring me. "I think they'll have a more dramatic effect, and you know Ms. Wiggins is all about the drama." She rolled her eyes. "I can't believe we're actually going to be graded on this! Life is so unfair."

I shot Hasenpfeffer a quick look, willing him to keep his mouth shut. "Listen, Darcy, something's come up. I can't work on the project today. I'm *really, really* sorry, but you need to go."

I held the door open, but she just stared at me. "What? You want *Maximilian Litmann* to get a better grade than us?"

"No, but this really isn't a good time."

"Maggie's right," Hasenpfeffer said. "You definitely need to go—even run! It's not safe to remain in the apartment," he said ominously. He looked all around. "I have firsthand information," he whispered, "from a ghost who told me that there's a *kobold* on the loose!"

Darcy put a hand on her hip. "I thought you said your rabbit was all better after that shape-shifter attack."

"He is."

"It sounds like that bite knocked a screw loose."

"No!" Hasenpfeffer said. "It's true! There was an actual ghost in the apartment today!"

"The rabbit is crackers," Darcy stated bluntly. She plopped herself down on the couch and started routing through her bag. "He's obviously emotionally scarred or suffering from some kind of post-traumatic stress disorder. I mean, seriously—a ghost? Pfff!"

Hasenpfeffer sat up on his haunches. "I am *not* crackers! I do have a few scars, but my fur hides them." He tilted his head down. "It does hide them, doesn't it?"

"Yes," I said tiredly.

"Good. But Maggie and I *have* been hearing voices

coming out of mirrors, and we've been seeing Milo's red cape flapping in the reflection too. I'm sorry I lied," he said to me, "but I was afraid your grandmother would dump me at the nearest shelter, and then . . ." He shuddered.

Darcy's lips turned up into a snarky smile. "Okay, so you're both crackers."

I sighed. "Like I said, this is a really bad time. You can call for a ride home; the phone is in the kitchen."

Hasenpfeffer chattered his teeth together. "I hate to say this, but from what the ghost said, we can use all the help we can get. Perhaps Darcy should stay? I'd feel much safer knowing there were two magicians protecting me."

"I don't think so," I said.

"What's a kobold, anyway?" Darcy asked.

Hasenpfeffer put his pink nose into the air. "Follow me." He started to hop down the hall to my bedroom, and we headed after him. "After the ghost came, I took it upon myself to do a little research on kobolds. I looked them up on the computer—not an easy thing to do with paws, I might add."

He jumped up onto my desk chair and jiggled the mouse with a paw until an article appeared on the computer screen. "It says here that kobolds are related to goblins and house brownies; though, one source said they were 'akin to leprechauns.' Depends on what you read. They're supposed to be rather helpful but have the potential to get quite nasty if you cross them."

He looked up at me. "According to your grandfather, we're dealing with the 'quite nasty' kind."

I shook my head. "Grandfather?"

"Yes," Hasenpfeffer said. "That would be the ghost I was talking about."

"My grandfather—Grandpa Malloy—was here in *ghost form*?" I asked.

Hasenpfeffer nodded. "The whole incident was rather upsetting. He gave me quite a start. I'm sure I'll have nightmares for months."

"Just tell me exactly what happened—exactly what my grandfather said."

Hasenpfeffer sighed. "Oh, I forgot—it's all about you. Who cares about *my* feelings? I'm just the one who was traumatized. I'm the one who was home alone not knowing if and when a nasty kobold might appear, and for all I know, rabbit might be their favorite thing to eat—"

"Just spit it out!" Darcy commanded. "I don't have all day."

Hasenpfeffer glared at her. "Fine." He cleared his throat. "The ghost was a little hard to follow, as he kept fading in and out. But, uh, let me think." He swung his head back and forth like a pendulum. "Okay," he said, jumping to the floor. "I was gnawing on the dresser when all of a sudden this *man* appeared in the middle of the room. I almost choked on a piece of wood!"

We both glanced over at the long gouge on one dresser leg.

"Just *nibbling*, really. Anyway, he was all panicked. Said you had to be warned about this kobold thingamajig. It seems your father acquired the kobold by accident when he was eleven. He bought a small wooden figure at an estate sale not knowing the creature came with it."

Suddenly Hasenpfeffer screamed. "He's back! Right over there by the closet!" he hollered as he dove into his cage and hid under his blanket. "Oh, I will have nightmares!"

Darcy and I turned around with a jump, as the temperature in the room rapidly dropped. Barely distinguishable by the light coming through the window, my grandfather's ghost hovered in a corner of my room.

"You must listen to me," he moaned.

Darcy gulped. "You know, maybe I will go home. We can work on our project when you're not so preoccupied."

"There's no time!" the ghost yelled. *"It's coming."*

"Or, I, uh, could st-st-stay," she whispered.

The ghost wrung his hands and sobbed. *"It's all my fault. Your father, Michael, was still so young—bursting with power—*

ful magic, magic he didn't fully understand. He was terribly unhappy and resented my refusal to use magic to better our situation."

I stared at the ghost. "Dad was 'bursting with power-ful magic'? What?"

"Didn't I tell you?" Hasenpfeffer called out from under his blanket. He poked his head out. "Gramps here told me your father is a powerful magician."

I looked back and forth between Hasenpfeffer and the ghost. "Dad? A magician?"

Darcy stared at me, openmouthed. "Wait. Everyone told me magic skipped a generation in your family."

I sat on the bed. "It did."

Hasenpfeffer chattered his teeth together. "Oh, it's a twisted tale if ever I've heard one. But magic *did not* skip a generation. Your father is a full-fledged, through-the-roof powerful magician. Only, he doesn't know it."

My head was spinning. "Dad . . . He can't be . . . He's not."

"It's true," the ghost said. *"And the kobold seemed to delight in Michael's anger. It goaded him to use his powers against others, including me. The creature's influence seemed to grow stronger each day—almost feeding off Michael's magic."*

My grandfather's ghost let out a tremendous moan that shook the glass in the window, and chills ran up my spine.

"Oh," he cried. "I only wanted to stop it before things got out of hand. But I rushed too fast, didn't do enough research, and the spell went horribly wrong. If only that had been the end, but . . ."

"But what?" I asked as my grandfather flickered in and out of view. "What happened?"

"I can't remain here much longer, but it's coming. Protect yourselves. Tell Mr. McGuire to find the wooden poppet. It's in the walls of the shop. Encase it in salt with a capture spell, and the kobold will be trapped again. Hurry. There may still be time . . ."

He suddenly vanished, and all I could hear was my labored breathing. "I don't believe this."

Darcy shook her head. "And I thought my family was messed up."

"Oh my, oh my!" Hasenpfeffer chattered from within his cage. "We'd better go to the shop. It's not safe here." He paused and then slowly crawled out from under his blanket. He cocked his head, and his pink eyes widened. "Did you hear something?"

Darcy and I looked around the room.

"I didn't hear anything," I said.

Hasenpfeffer's ears twitched. "Listen."

I heard the front door shut softly.

"Is your grandmother home?" Darcy asked nervously.

I shook my head. "I don't think so; she stays late at the food pantry on Fridays, making sure people have food for the weekend, and besides, I would've heard her keys jangling in the lock."

"Hello?" a gravelly voice called out.

"Who is that?" I whispered as goose bumps peppered my arms.

Darcy looked at me with wide eyes and shrugged.

"Maggie?" the voice rasped out. "I just want to talk. No need to be throwing magic around. I just want to talk and make sure I'm not making a mistake."

My stomach dropped, and I called out, "Who—who are you, and how do you know my name?"

"I've been listening to you in the repair shop for a while now—biding my time until I could be free from my prison. I've spent years waiting. It's tempting to just strike out and take my revenge, but I am an honorable creature."

"It's the kobold! Lock the door!" Hasenpfeffer wailed.

I raced to shut my bedroom door. "It doesn't have a lock!"

"You don't need to be afraid of me," the creature called out. "Not yet anyway. It all depends on you."

"Lock the door—use magic!" Hasenpfeffer pleaded as he ran around in circles. "What are you waiting for?"

I ran to my desk and pulled my wand out of a drawer. I pointed it toward the door with a shaking hand. "I—I can't think of a spell."

"Don't lock it," the creature beseeched, and I heard tiny footsteps rushing closer to my room.

"Hurry, you idiot!" Darcy yelled.

"Um . . ." I hopped up and down on my feet. "Okay. *On the outside, don't let him in. Lock this door so we're safe within.*"

A yellow light shot out of the tip of my wand and circled the doorknob a few times, and then a keyhole appeared. An audible click sounded, and I lowered my wand, swallowing hard. "We should be okay."

"Took you long enough!" Darcy panted.

"You could've locked the door too, you know!"

Her pale, freckled cheeks reddened. "Sorry, but I'm a little freaked out. I wasn't expecting a homicidal kobold to be breaking into your apartment!" she snapped.

The doorknob turned, and the kobold shook the door. "I asked you not to lock it." He pounded on the wood. "You didn't need to go and do that. This makes me very angry."

There was a pause, and then the creature cleared his throat. "I'm sorry. It's just that I've been cooped up so long, and here I am offering you a chance . . . but you're just a wee thing. I know you must be scared, but you don't have to be. It's not what you think."

"I think the fact that my grandfather felt the need to come back from the dead and warn me about you is not a good sign!"

"Don't mention that man to me!" the kobold said angrily. "Your dad and I were friends—for a while," he continued more calmly. "I tried to help him, really I did, but I'm thinking maybe we can be friends."

"Go away!" I yelled. "We are *never* going to be friends!"

"Are you sure we can't talk?" the kobold called through the door. "Think hard about this, for your decision can lead to dire consequences for you."

"Oh, give it up," a voice said behind me. "I told you she's just as bad as the rest of them. You should have trusted me."

I twirled around, and my blood ran cold. Staring out at me from my bedroom mirror was Milo the Magnificent. His arms were folded across his chest while his red cape flapped around him.

"Wh-what are you doing here?" I cried.

"Cousin Milo!" Darcy said. "It's me, Darcy!"

Milo narrowed his eyes. "Darcy? Fraternizing with the enemy? How utterly disappointing."

Darcy shook her head. "No! I'm only here for a school project."

"Well, then, I suggest you go home now," Milo said, "before you get sucked into our game."

My hand tightened around my wand. "Game?" I asked. "What are you talking about?"

Milo's lips turned up into a snaky smile. "The game of revenge. Are we ready, my good friend?"

"Yes," the kobold called out. "You were right, Milo. The Malloys are a selfish lot who don't see what's really going on around them—making others pay for their arrogance and ignorance."

"Habanero!" Milo called out. "You know what to do!"

In a flash of blinding light, a small red dragon with a thin snakelike body flew out of the mirror and hovered in the air. His body was the size of a large cat, and he had what looked like an orange mustache and beard. He blew out a thin stream of fiery breath, making my nose sting and my eyes water as I breathed in the peppery smell.

The dragon dove toward us, and Darcy and I threw ourselves onto the floor.

"Help!" Darcy wailed.

The dragon flew around my room, spewing spicy flames as he went.

"Stop showing off, you leather-winged nitwit," Milo commanded. "Just grab the rabbit and bring it to me!"

Hasenpfeffer squealed as the dragon dipped down toward him—five claws on each foot extended. The dragon latched on to the scruff of Hasenpfeffer's neck and lifted him into the air. "Maggie! Help me!"

I scrambled to my feet, but before I could point my wand, the dragon flew into the mirror with Hasenpfeffer. "No! Come back!" I screamed. I raced to the mirror, and Milo smiled with an evil glint in his eyes.

"Two down. One to go," he said, pulling on his long mustache. "I'll be seeing you soon!" He snapped his fingers and disappeared, leaving only my worried reflection staring back at me.

"It's done, then," the kobold called out from the other side of the door. "But . . . perhaps if we could talk—face-to-face. I've listened to you so often in the shop, and I'm not convinced Milo is right about you. I'm not sure you should be punished for what happened to me." He paused. "Don't be alarmed, but I'm coming in."

I heard a scraping noise on the door as if the creature's fingers were tracing the knob. I knew I should do something, but the grinding in my ears kept me spellbound. Suddenly the noise stopped and I heard a click, like a key turning in a lock.

"It broke your spell!" Darcy whispered frantically. "It's coming in!"

We both backed away from the door, wands raised.

The knob turned, and the door slowly opened. "I just want to talk. *Please,*" the creature said.

I grabbed Darcy's hand. *"I wish we were at the repair shop!"* I yelled.

I blinked and caught a glimpse of a brown gnarled hand with black clawlike fingernails curling around my door. We had just enough time to scream before the magic swept us away.

6
Three Is
a Magic Number

Darcy and I materialized on the sidewalk above the repair shop—right in front of Raphael and Fiona.

"I feel sick," Darcy moaned.

Raphael jumped out of the way, clutching his chest. "Aaahh! You scared me half to death!"

"Maggie!" Fiona said. "We were just taking a break from our project, and I wanted to visit Mr. McGuire. Are you taking a break too?

"No time to talk," I said breathlessly as I started down the steps. "Milo is back and he has a creature with him and they have Hasenpfeffer!"

"What? Milo is back?" Fiona asked as she hurried down after me. "And what happened to Hasenpfeffer?"

I opened the door. "Apparently some creature called a kobold escaped from wherever my grandfather trapped it, and it has teamed up with Milo. And it turns out my father is a—"

I stopped short, and Fiona, Raphael, and Darcy bumped into me. The magic mirror was standing in a corner of the shop with dozens of flower-covered vines snaking out of it onto the floor and up the shelves. Butterflies with mirrored wings flitted through the air, occasionally landing on some of the red fragrant flowers.

"Oh no," Raphael groaned.

Fiona stretched out her arm as a butterfly flitted by.

"Be careful!" he said sharply, slapping at her hand. "It could be dangerous."

Darcy laughed. "What's the matter? Are you scared of a few flowers and butterflies, Raphael?"

"No, but statically speaking I think the odds of these turning out to be harmless vines and butterflies are zero to one."

"I'm going to have to agree with Raphael," I said. "After what just happened in my room, we need to be extra careful," I said.

Darcy scoffed and took a step toward the mirror.

"Stop!" I said, tugging on her arm. "Last time Raphael and I found the mirror acting strangely, we fell in and were almost eaten by crocodiles. But go ahead if you want a closer look."

She wrinkled her nose and took a step back. "Okay. Well, let's hurry up and find Mr. McGuire so he can get your rabbit and we can start working on our project."

"There's a kobold on the loose and Hasenpfeffer was just kidnapped. The project is the last thing on my mind! Mr. McGuire?" I called out.

"Uh-oh. Maggie, look," Fiona said. "In the vines coming out of the top of the mirror."

I followed her gaze and saw a pair of glasses with thick lenses coiled tightly in the vines. My heart sank. "Those are Mr. McGuire's. After that dragon took Hasenpfeffer, Milo did say 'Two down. One to go.' They must have grabbed him, too." I nibbled nervously on my lip. "I guess it's up to us to rescue both of them now."

Darcy cocked her head. "'Us'? There is no 'us.'"

"Yes, there is," Fiona insisted. "We'll all help you find them."

"Count me out," Darcy said. "For starters I'm not a huge fan of dragons or creepy little kobolds." She turned to Fiona. "That thing had black fingernails!"

Fiona's eyes popped. "Dragons?"

"Milo sent a small dragon after Hasenpfeffer, and then it carried him away through my bedroom mirror."

Raphael wrinkled his brow. "I think you need to fill us in from the beginning, and then we can decide who to call for help. I'm going to have to side with Darcy on this one. From what I'm hearing, this doesn't sound like something a bunch of kids should be messing with."

I looked up at Mr. McGuire's glasses just as a butterfly land on them. "You're probably right. We need some outside help. Darcy, will you write to Viola Klemp? There's a mailbox hanging on the wall behind the counter. I'll fill Raphael and Fiona in on what happened."

Darcy sighed impatiently. "Fine. Maybe Viola can send some people to rescue Mr. McGuire and your rabbit so we can get some work done."

I shook my head. "Doesn't trying to be number one all the time get tiring?"

She smirked. "No. It just comes naturally."

While Darcy wrote to Viola Klemp, I told Raphael and Fiona about my grandfather's ghost, the kobold, and Milo sending the dragon after Hasenpfeffer. "So from what he said, it sounds like my grandfather trapped the kobold by sealing up some carved figure it's magically bound to in a block of salt, and then he stashed it in the walls of the shop."

I looked around, trying to figure out where the poppet might be hidden. "It could be anywhere—behind the shelves or in some sort of secret compartment. We'll have to use a spell to locate it, and we need to find out what a 'capture' spell is. My grandfather said that will trap the kobold again."

"Maggie," Fiona said, "maybe your grandmother knows where it is. We could call her."

"No, she . . ." I stopped. After Mr. McGuire had brought us back from Scotland at four o'clock in the morning and told Gram about the magical mayhem that had gone on—and that Raphael and Fiona would have to stay overnight—Gram had sighed and said it was like living with my father all over again. She'd looked startled to hear the words come out of her mouth and had quickly rattled off something about my father always having sleepovers. And there was her reaction this morning when I told her about the voices, and she'd said something about my father then too. Now I realized she was referring to the fact that Dad was a magician.

"She knows," I said. "She knows my father is a magician. But why didn't she tell me? And what happened to my father that made him forget?"

A loud hissing noise pierced the air, and I saw steam pouring out of the mailbox. "I sent the letter," Darcy said.

She walked around the counter and then gasped, pointing toward the floor. "Fiona, look out!"

I turned just in time to see a vine rapidly snake up Fiona's leg and yank her toward the mirror.

"Help!" she shrieked as more vines reached out and twisted around her arms and chest. Tendrils engulfed her, pulling at her hair and unraveling her braids as she struggled and screamed.

Raphael and I raced toward the mirror. The glass butterflies blew up in puffs of red smoke, revealing angry hornets the size of golf balls that zipped toward us as the leaves and flowers disappeared from the vines. Sharp thorns poked out, and spiky creepers lashed out at us, driving us behind the counter.

Milo appeared from within the glass, his eyes blazing with glee. "Come, my pets!" he called out. "We have our quarry."

The hornets turned direction and zipped through the glass. A spiky vine gave one last thump on the counter, and then the lot retracted back into the mirror—with Fiona still in their clutches.

Fog poured out of the glass in their wake, and as it cleared, a wooden door surrounded by high walls appeared in the reflection.

Raphael stood up and leaned on the counter, breathing hard. He yanked a large green thorn out of the top of the counter and then turned his head toward Darcy, who was cowering on the floor. "*This* is why I was afraid of the flowers and the butterflies," he said, waving the thorn around.

Darcy nodded, her eyes wide and frightened as she pulled herself up.

Suddenly the castle door swung open with a creak. We ducked down until our eyes were level with the counter so we could see what was happening. Milo the Magnificent stood in the doorway on the other side of the glass, a mocking smile on his face. Habanero the dragon sat perched on his shoulder, and a white cat sat at his feet.

The cat leapt out of the mirror, and as it landed on the repair shop floor, it grew and changed until a small, wrinkled man no more than two feet tall appeared in its place. The man was dressed in plain simple brown clothes, and pointed ears poked out from his messy dark hair. He clutched a rolled-up piece of parchment with tiny hands studded with black clawlike nails.

"The kobold," Darcy whispered with a quaking voice.

"You!" I said angrily. "You were the white cat that was hanging around. What were you doing? Spying on me?"

"Actually, yes," the kobold stated matter-of-factly. "I

was gathering information so my friend and I could finalize our plans."

"Plans that took forever to come to fruition," Milo muttered.

The kobold narrowed his dark eyes as he looked over his shoulder at Milo, who was still in the mirror. "I told you a hundred times, I wanted to make sure everything was perfect."

Milo waved a hand dismissively in the air. "Yes, yes, so you keep saying. Let's carry on, shall we?"

The kobold turned back to me. "Your grandfather unjustly imprisoned me for thirty-four years, and it is now time to take my revenge upon your family!"

I put a hand on my hip. *"Unjustly?"*

"Yes!" the creature hissed. "Once I was freed, I disguised myself as a cat to avoid detection. I was almost discovered by Mr. McGuire, but I ran into the back room and slipped behind the sheet covering the mirror."

"If you went behind the cover, you must have been sucked in," I said.

The kobold nodded. "It was inside the mirror that I met poor Milo, cowering in a windswept fog with leach-like creatures hanging from his cape. He told me how you trapped him in the mirror while he was trying to *save* you."

"That's a lie!" I shouted, pointing to Milo. "He wasn't

trying to save me. He was trying to get his duplicate in the mirror, and he didn't care if I was going in too! It was his own fault he ended up in there."

Milo laughed coldly. "I told you she'd say that, didn't I? These Malloys are all alike. Liars and cheats."

The kobold scowled at me. "Yes, I agree wholeheartedly. Now, let's get down to business. Unlike your grandfather, I am a member of the Fay, and as such I'm bound by the rules of fair play. As is tradition in the fairy world, you must perform three tasks. If you are successful, you and your friends will be set free. If you fail, I will release Milo from the mirror and you will take his place—forever."

I shook my head. "Everyone who's investigated the mirror said Milo can't be set free, so this whole thing is pointless."

"Fairies and their kind are among the most powerful creatures in the world," Milo said. "With his power we've already opened up countless realms in the mirror and created a vast kingdom where I could spy on you from every mirror you looked into." Milo puffed out his chest and threw out his arms. "Just call me the Master of Mirrors."

Habanero wobbled on his shoulders. The dragon flapped his wings and blew out a stream of red flames. Milo dissolved into a fit of coughing as tears poured down his face. He swatted at the dragon. "Get away from me, you pepper-breathing pea-brained lizard. Go to the house and get ready to heat up the oven." He laughed. "Rabbit is on the menu today!"

"No!" I cried as the dragon cowered and then flew out of sight.

"Don't worry," the kobold said. "The rabbit is safe—for now—but saving him is your first task."

"This is ridiculous," Darcy said. "If you're so powerful, why don't you just free Milo and skip all this nonsense?"

"Well . . ." The kobold looked uneasily back at Milo. "It wouldn't be fair if I just set him free without his earning it, now, would it?"

Milo rolled his eyes. "Yes, yes, everything must be *by the book*—everything must be *fair*. There must be three tasks. Three is a magic number." He waved his hands in the air. "Blah, blah, blah."

From the sour-lemon look on Milo's face, it was obvious he and the kobold had discussed the matter at length, and not to Milo's satisfaction. Milo may have been calling himself 'the Master of Mirrors,' but it was clear that the kobold was running the show.

"How is it fair that Milo can earn his freedom without completing any tasks?" Raphael asked.

The kobold smiled, revealing oversize yellowed, crooked teeth. "Oh, but he did. I came up with the ideas for the challenges, but Milo's task was to make them difficult to complete."

"And I'm very much looking forward to seeing how you handle the special touches I added to all three challenges," Milo said.

"Enough chatter," the kobold said. "My patience is not infinite, and I'm anxious to begin."

He unfurled the parchment, and I saw it was covered on both sides with some indecipherable writing I figured must be fairy language, but at the bottom my name was clearly written in thick bloodred ink.

The kobold's eyes traced the page, and then he looked up. "Everything seems to be in order. You may use any magic at your disposal except the power to transport yourself. That is strictly prohibited, as you could easily take yourself out of the mirror. Not that I imagine you'd want to abandon your friends. Now you may choose one person to help you on your quest. Choose wisely; your success or failure could depend on it."

I turned to Raphael. He grimaced and his shoulders slumped, but he nodded, letting me know he would go if I asked him.

"You *better* not pick me," Darcy stated.

I scoffed. "Darcy, you're the *last* person—"

"Done!" the kobold said, and Darcy's name appeared next to mine on the parchment.

"No, no, no! Wait!" Darcy protested. "She didn't pick me."

I bobbed my head rapidly up and down. "Yeah, I *totally* did not pick her!"

"You said her name, and now it's on the contract. If she refuses to go, you will automatically forfeit the game and the two of you will immediately be banished to the dungeon, where you will live out your lives with our other captives."

I glared at Darcy. "She'll do it. *Right, Darcy?*"

"Wait, Milo, isn't there any way you can get me out of this?" Darcy pleaded. "We're family!"

Milo sighed and smiled at her sympathetically. "Oh, I do wish I could help. *Truly* I do, but alas—your name is on an unbreakable contract. While I regret that I shall be praying for your failure, when the inevitable happens and you are stuck in the mirror, I will do my utmost to see that you get preferential treatment and perhaps a soft pillow and blanket in the dungeon."

Darcy glowered at him. "Thanks for your help, but when Maggie and I *win*, I'll do my utmost not to cry when you're left to rot in that stinking mirror. And you can be sure I'll tell Viola Klemp to stop looking for a way to get you out!"

The kobold nodded. "Very good, then. Let's get started." He snapped his fingers, and the parchment disappeared with a crack. "You have five minutes to prepare, after which the door will reopen and it will be time to begin. Milo, let's make sure all is in order." He rubbed his hands together. "This should be fun!"

The kobold shrank back into the white cat and padded his way back to the mirror. The cat turned and regarded us, twitched his whiskers, and then leapt back through the glass. Milo turned with a flounce of his cape, and the door slammed shut.

Darcy got up in my face and started yelling. "*I cannot believe you got me into this mess.* Just *wait* until my mother finds out. You are in so much trouble! And if I get trapped in that stupid mirror forever, I will *kill* you!"

"I was all set to choose *Raphael*! If you hadn't said 'You better not pick me,' I wouldn't have said your name out loud!" I shot back.

"Cut it out!" Raphael yelled. "You have only five minutes to get ready, and arguing is not helping anything."

I clenched my jaw as my chest heaved up and down. "You're right. Raphael, you'll need to call my grandmother at the food pantry and tell her what's happened.

Tell her we need to find the kobold's poppet. Get in touch with Franny; her number is on the wall by the phone. Maybe she can give us some information about dealing with dragons.

"Oh, and tell them we need to find a capture spell to trap the kobold with his poppet. And be on the lookout for a reply from Viola Klemp. She may be able to get in touch with some other people who can help too."

"How will I be able to talk to you?" he asked.

"Uh." My brow furrowed. "Through a mirror! If Milo can do it, so can I."

I took out the compact mirror I'd been carrying around and put it on the counter. "I read about an elementary duplicating spell in a book Sir Lachlan gave me when I was preparing for my World Federation of Magic test. If I tweak it, I think we'll be able to communicate."

I held my wand over the compact as my mind raced to come up with just the right words. "Okay, I think I have it. *Reverse the reflection, times it by two. Raphael to Maggie, expand our view.*"

A flash of blue came out of my wand, and instantly a duplicate compact appeared. I grabbed them both and handed one to Raphael. "Cross your fingers."

I opened the compact and smiled to see Raphael staring back at me.

"Can you hear me?" he said, his voice echoing out of the small mirror.

I beamed at his reflection. "Yes! Can you see and hear me?"

"Loud and clear!"

Suddenly trumpets blared from within the magic mirror, and I jumped.

"Time must be almost up," I said quietly.

"Be careful, Maggie," Raphael said. He tilted his head toward Darcy who was staring at the mirror. "Don't let Darcy get you mad. You need to stay focused," he said quietly.

My stomach fluttered like I'd swallowed a hundred butterflies. "I'll try."

I turned to Darcy. Her lips were pursed and her wand hand was trembling.

"Can you have someone call my mother, Raphael?" she asked in a quavering voice. "Tell her that I . . . you know."

Raphael nodded.

The door in the mirror swung open, and brown dirt tumbled out, forming a rough path. In the mirror I could see that the path cut through a field of red flowers leading to the edge of a forest. "We can do this, Darcy. I know it."

She bent over and picked up Mr. McGuire's glasses that were now lying on the floor at the base of the mirror. She tucked them into her shirt pocket and then turned to me with narrowed eyes. "We'd better. Or I will do everything in my power to make your life in that mirror *miserable*."

7

Sugar Plums
and Peppers

We stepped through the door into the magic mirror, and a round yellow sun blazed above us. A hot breeze blew across the field, making the sea of red tulips bow our way like a welcome, bolstering my confidence. Here and there turrets jutted out of the forest of tall pines, and beyond the trees, a castle sat sentry on a hill. Red striped poles were posted every six feet or so along the path, each sporting a red banner bearing Milo's leering face.

"Milo always was a bit full of himself," Darcy muttered.

Cracked mirror fragments of all shapes and sizes stood upright along the path like teeth, and I saw myself endlessly reflected. A few mirrors peppered along the forest's edge made sure we'd stay on the path—though it looked like the path forked here and there.

"It's like a maze," I said.

Suddenly the door swung shut behind us, and dozens of keyholes appeared on it, clicking and clacking as they locked us in.

"Why is it so hot and sticky?" Darcy grumbled. "My hair is frizzing, isn't it?"

"It looks fine," I lied.

"Hey, what's wrong with your shadow?"

I looked down and saw that my shadow was glinting in the sun like it had been infused with gold dust. "Oh, I swallowed a potion yesterday to help with a repair job. Mr. McGuire told me it would wear off soon; we tried a bunch of different spells, but apparently it hasn't yet.

"How could having a glittery shadow possibly fix anything?"

"Actually, it was just supposed to be my reflection that needed to shine—you know, like a lure—for a ghost croc. But I was given an adult dose, and this is one of the side effects."

Darcy laughed. "Seriously? A ghost croc?"

I folded my arms across my chest. "Yes. Do you have a problem with that?"

"No." She snorted. "But you magic repair people sure do know how to have fun."

"It wasn't fun! I almost got killed. But at least I saved a little boy from dying. What did *you* do yesterday?"

Darcy kicked a stone on the path. "I did a lot of . . . Forget it," she said sullenly. She picked up speed, and I jogged to catch up with her.

"Hey, you know Milo pretty well, right?" I asked.

"Sort of," she answered as she continued walking.

"Well, if we know his weaknesses, we might be able to use them to our advantage. I know he's afraid of insects. Can you think of anything else?"

"I usually stayed in my room when he was over. He never shut up about his shows and how much his fans adored him." Darcy rolled her eyes. "Does being a pompous jerk who always needs to be number one count as a weakness?"

"Apparently it runs in the family." The second the words came out of my mouth, I wished I could magic them away.

Darcy stopped short and turned to me, her hands on her hips. "I don't always need to be number one!"

I raised one eyebrow. "Oh, come on! You're stuck in

this stupid mirror with me because you couldn't stand the thought that Max and Serena might get a better grade on a five-minute *puppet* show."

Darcy's cheeks fired up—matching the color of the tulips in the field. "I'm just so sick of Ms. Wiggins going all gaga over Max's stupid haikus. And *Fiona* is such a 'blossoming star' because she's into saving baby animals. And you . . . "

Darcy's face screwed up, and I thought she might burst from frustration.

"Hey, we're all 'blossoming stars' in our own way," I said in Ms. Wiggins's voice, hoping to lighten the mood. "And it's okay that you're an overachiever. It's who you are. And it's okay if you're not Ms. Wiggins's favorite. We can't all be the teacher's pet."

Darcy scoffed and started walking again. "I've never been anyone's favorite," she said quietly. "Ever."

I didn't know what to say to that. We all knew Max was a big, goofy marshmallow, and Darcy was a prickly pear with a DO NOT TOUCH sticker on it. The one thing that surprised me was that Darcy was actually bothered by this.

"Let me check in with Raphael," I said, changing the subject.

I opened my compact, and Raphael appeared, his face filled with worry. "Hey, Raphael, what's going on?"

"What's going on is that I'm relieved to talk to you!" Raphael said. "I thought you'd check in right away."

"Sorry. We had a few, uh, things to work out."

"Okay, I talked to your grandmother; she's stuck in traffic but will be here as soon as possible. The good news is she knows where your grandfather put the block of salt he trapped the kobold's poppet in. If we can get it, and get someone to retrap it again, the contract with your name on it might be null and void."

"That's great news!" I smiled for the first time since this nightmare had started, thinking we just might make it out of the mirror after all.

"Franny is on her way, and Viola Klemp wrote back and she's gathering a crew to help. Have you started your first task?" he asked.

"Not yet. We're almost to the edge of the forest. I have a feeling we'll find out what it is soon."

"Maggie!" Darcy squealed. "Is that the thing you were talking about—that . . . that *ghost croc*?"

I turned around, and my heart thudded in my chest. A white crocodile had just finished clumping out of a mirror fragment. "Uh—uh," I stuttered. "That would be Buhodu. Mr. McGuire trapped it in the mirror, and I guess with the kobold playing around with the mirror's realms, Buhodu got loose in this one."

Buhodu looked up and down the path, and then his ghostly eyes locked onto mine. He opened his jaws, let out a low guttural roar, and then started toward us with a hopping gait.

Darcy raced up the path. "Run!"

"Maggie, are you still there?" Raphael asked from within the compact.

"Raphael! Can crocodiles outrun humans?" I asked, hustling after Darcy toward the forest.

"No, but you should move in a straight line; it's a myth that crocodiles can't run in a zigzag line," he said. "Why do you ask?"

"Because Buhodu is after us! Gotta go!"

I snapped the compact shut and stuffed it into my back pocket. "Wands out!" I yelled.

I looked over my shoulder and threw some zaps of electrifying magic toward him, but it had no effect. Buhodu just picked up speed and roared again.

"I hate that stupid ghost croc!" I shouted. "The magic isn't doing anything to him."

"He's following your shadow!" Darcy yelled.

I pointed my wand toward a mirror standing along the path. *"Illuminate!"* I shouted.

The mirror burst with light, and I peeked over my shoulder again to see Buhodu slow as he approached it.

The crocodile stopped, lifted his snout into the air, and sniffed. He then trundled into the fragment, seemingly mesmerized by the glow, and disappeared.

"Great," I said. "So now we have to worry about a ghost croc in addition to the three tasks. This just keeps getting better and better."

"Can he really hurt us?" Darcy asked breathlessly. "I mean, he's just a ghost, right?"

I looked her in the eye. "He can *kill* you."

Darcy's bottom lip quivered. "I want to go home. I want my mother."

I bowed my head. "Me too." My mother was thousands of miles away, and I might never get to see her again. And my father—well, there were a million questions I had about him, the biggest being why he'd befriended this horrible kobold in the first place.

Darcy cocked her head over her shoulder. "Let's keep going before that thing finds its way out and comes after us again."

We were at a juncture, and I looked up each path. "Let's head into the forest. I shouldn't have much of a shadow there."

"Your shadow may be the least of our problems in the forest."

I looked ahead at the tall, dark pine trees towering

over the path and saw the white cat peek out from a low branch. It quickly ducked out of sight.

"Did you see that?" I whispered.

"Yes, and if that thing is skulking around, I'm thinking we're close to our first task."

I let out a long breath. "Let's go see what it is."

We headed into the woods, and the air cooled. After a few minutes the path forked again and we stopped. "Which way?" I asked.

"I say we go that way," Darcy said, hitching a thumb at the white cat lurking in the ferns about twenty feet up to the left.

"And look," I said, pointing to a line of small white stones that seemed to glow in the gloom. "Does that remind you of anything?"

Darcy rolled her eyes and groaned. "Not *Hansel and Gretel* again?"

"That would explain the oven Milo was talking about." I shuddered. "I'm not looking forward to meeting the witch."

Five minutes later we turned a corner, and the forest opened up to reveal a partially constructed cottage. The front of the house was missing, and it reminded me of the lean-to I'd slept in at a campground once. Giant chocolate chip cookies hung like shingles on the roof, and sugar plums dotted the gingerbread walls. I pulled Darcy off the path, and we crept softly between the mirrors so we could get a better look at what we were up against, and hopefully avoid detection.

Large striped candy canes poked out of a garden at odd angles. Peppermint, ginger, and powdered sugar smells wafted around us. As we got closer, I could see Hasenpfeffer sitting in a cage dangling from a thick chain, just inches above a large cast-iron stove. The oven door was open, and the inside was filled with brush and small sticks that were ready to be ignited.

I scanned the area for any sign of the white cat or Milo, but the only things in the area were more mirror fragments jutting out of the ground or propped up against trees.

"We have to be very, very careful or Hasenpfeffer is toast!" I said in a hushed voice. I shook my head. "What kind of diabolic creature would do something like that to an innocent rabbit?"

"Apparently, a homicidal kobold and my cousin Milo would," Darcy said bitterly.

We inched our way closer, and I could hear Hasenpfeffer talking.

"So, there I was sitting on the floor of the magic repair shop, still utterly traumatized from being duplicated, and he says, 'As for that repellent rodent, I won't have him sullying my reputation again. You can use him for hasenpfeffer for all I care.' And then he up and *leaves me* with complete strangers! I was terrified I'd be dumped on the street and have to forage in garbage bins for food if—if I wasn't eaten by feral cats first!"

"Who is he talking to?" Darcy whispered.

I narrowed my eyes but couldn't see anyone else in the house. "I don't know. The witch? Hansel and Gretel?"

Hasenpfeffer chattered his teeth angrily. "Rodent! I mean, of all the things to call a rabbit. It's absolutely insulting."

A trilling bell-like noise came from within the house.

"I know. It was probably the worst thing Milo could have said to me. And after years of loyal service! I'm positive it's because he was jealous of me. I was the real star of the act. You should have heard the applause when I came out of the hat every night. Oh, if only you could've seen me; I just lit up the stage with star power. But did that earn me any respect?"

More trills.

"Exactly! None whatsoever. And if you're wise, you'll learn from my woeful tale and get me out of this cage and we can escape this place together. Milo is not someone you can trust."

A series of chirps and sharp whistles burst from the house.

Hasenpfeffer sighed. "Well, if you let me go before anyone shows up, Milo will never know it was you who freed me. And like I said, you can come live with me. There is a grouchy old lady to deal with, but she works a lot, and I'm sure Maggie would be happy to magic up as many hot peppers as you'd like."

Darcy and I exchanged looks and shrugged.

"Think it over. Live with me and my servant girl, or be at the mercy of Milo and that dreadful little kobold. You need to decide quickly, though. I heard the trumpets blaring, and the kobold said that meant the game was about to start. The lot of them could show up at any minute and . . ." Hasenpfeffer sniffed. "You could be forced to light the fire."

A purring trill sang out.

"Oh, you're too kind," Hasenpfeffer replied with a quaking voice. "I don't know what I did to deserve such a friend as you." He sat up and put his paws on the bars of the cage. "But remember, it's the spiky dandelion leaves I like best. It's not parsley, but it'll do in a pinch."

Suddenly the small dragon, Habanero, flew out from the cottage rafters and off into the woods.

"I don't think there *is* a witch!" I cried. "I think they

put that dragon in the house instead. I'll bet we're supposed to fight him before he can light the fire and cook Hasenpfeffer. We need to get him out of there before Habanero comes back."

A glint of determination flickered in Darcy's eyes. "We're getting that rabbit if it's the last thing we do! Now, move out!"

We dashed toward the house, and Hasenpfeffer squealed with delight. "Thank goodness you're here! Milo's set me up to be roasted. Oh, but I do have some good news. I've adopted a dragon! Well, it's more like I'm his *mentor*, but do you think your grandmother will mind?"

"Let's get you out of here first, and then we can discuss your dragon guru gig when you're safe!" I turned the cage around, looking for a door, only to find there wasn't one. "There's no way to open it."

"There's probably some magic key to open it," Darcy said.

"Yes!" Hasenpfeffer said. "I remember overhearing them talking about how hard it would be to find the key, and how it was likely I'd be cooked first." He froze for a second and then wailed. "You need to find it, and fast! Habanero will listen to me if Milo isn't here, but if he shows up, I'm roasted for sure!"

"Uh-oh," Darcy said. "Dragon at two o'clock."

I turned to see Habanero hovering in the air, bunches of dandelion leaves clutched in his long red talons. The dragon narrowed his yellow eyes, screeched, and let out a stream of hot flames. Darcy and I jumped aside and dashed out of the cottage, choking on the burnt hair and pepper smell that filled the air.

As we retreated to the edge of the forest, the dragon flew in and latched his back claws onto Hasenpfeffer's cage. He stuffed the leaves inside the bars and then hissed in our direction.

"Ha-Habanero!" Hasenpfeffer sputtered and coughed. "Stop that; I can hardly breathe! And they were only trying to help!"

Habanero hung his head and cooed mournfully.

"I know you're scared," Hasenpfeffer said. He sat up in the cage and rubbed his paws over his watering eyes. "But these are the good guys—well, one of them is anyway."

Habanero let out a long string of trills, chirps, and agitated grunts.

"It's Milo's fault there will be a battle. Not Maggie's!" Hasenpfeffer answered back. "And I don't want you to fight them, especially the one with the frizzy hair! You could get hurt."

"Hey!" Darcy protested. "That's getting personal!"

The dragon opened his wings, glided down, and wrapped his claws on the top of a candy cane just in front of the cottage. He looked back at Hasenpfeffer and then eyed us suspiciously. He stretched out his wings and let loose another volley of peppery flames our way.

"Keep watch, Darcy," I said, ducking behind a tree. "I'll see if Raphael can help." I opened my mirror, and Raphael appeared. "How's it going?" he asked.

"We're having a bit of a standoff with Milo's dragon. Were you able to get in touch with Franny?"

"Right here," Franny called out. Her face appeared in the compact, and she raised both eyebrows. "You are just a magnet for trouble, aren't you, kiddo?"

"I guess so," I said, but just seeing her made me feel better.

Franny pushed her red curls out of her face. "Hang in there, Maggie. The cavalry is on its way. That kobold has an ironclad lock on the mirror, but Sir Lachlan and Lyra are researching ways to break it, and Viola is rounding up a team of experts. Everyone is convinced that sealing the kobold's poppet in salt again will take him out of the picture. So as soon as your grandmother arrives, we'll get started on that. Milo is the big question mark, but if we take the kobold out, his powers in the mirror should greatly diminish."

"That's good to know. Did Raphael ask you about dragons?"

"He did, but they've been extinct for hundreds of years. I only know what I've read in books."

"They're not all extinct."

I pointed the compact toward the gingerbread cottage and heard Franny squeal. "Look at him! He looks just like the pictures of Chinese dragons I've seen, but it's rare to see one with wings. Oh, he's beautiful!"

I brought the mirror back behind the tree and held out some of my hair that had been singed at the bottom. "He's not so beautiful when he's trying to fry you!"

"Right," Franny said. "Let's see. From what I've read, the driving force behind dragons—and most animals—is food. You know the old saying: The way to a dragon's heart is through its stomach."

I smiled. "I think I know what this little guy likes to eat. Wish me luck!"

"Good luck, kiddo. Be careful, and know we are doing everything we can to get to you."

Tears pooled in my eyes. "Thanks, Franny. That means a lot." I shut the compact and turned to Darcy. "Can you magic us up some peppers?" She wrinkled her nose. "Peppers?"

"Yes! The hotter the better."

8

Cobwebs and Keys

Darcy cast a spell, and a basket of red and green peppers appeared on the ground.

"Do you really think it will work?" she asked.

"Franny is a magical animal expert, so I trust her. But will you watch my back with your wand, just in case?"

She nodded.

I picked up the basket and slowly came out from behind the tree I was hiding behind.

"Hey there, little buddy. I have some treats for you," I cooed.

"There. That's Maggie," Hasenpfeffer called out. "She's

the one I was telling you about. Just ignore the other one, but Maggie is a kind and gentle servant—er, uh, I mean master."

Habanero craned his long neck toward me.

I took one step toward the cottage, holding the basket out in front of me. "Do you like peppers? I have some. They're nice and hot. You like them hot, don't you?"

Habanero leaned forward, and his nostrils flared as he sniffed the air. He bobbed his head up and down as his mouth curved up to reveal a toothy grin.

I tilted my head back to where Darcy was. "My friend Darcy got these just for you."

I looked behind to see Darcy step out from behind a tree, with her wand raised and a smile on her face. Habanero began to whine like a dog.

"Put the wand down," I told her.

Darcy nodded and stuck the wand into her back pocket.

"It's okay," Hasenpfeffer said. "She's—*They're* good people. They won't hurt you."

"That's right. We're not going to hurt you," Darcy said. "Even if that's what Milo and the kobold want us to do."

"Come on, boy." I picked up a deep red pepper and swung it back and forth as I slowly approached the dragon. "Here's a nice juicy pepper just for you."

I tossed the pepper into the air, and Habanero flapped his wings and soared up to snatch it. He swooped down to the cottage roof and gobbled the pepper up.

I threw another up, and Habanero glided down and grabbed it with his claws and then ate it as he hovered.

"Let me try," Darcy said.

I handed her a pepper and she tossed it over her head. Habanero trilled and swooped up and then landed on the ground ten feet from us. I put the basket on the ground and motioned for Darcy to take a few steps back.

"You can have as many as you want," I said.

Habanero's lips drew back in a reptilian smile. He made a croaking noise much like a frog and then weaved around the candy canes to the basket. He sniffed the peppers and examined several before picking a long twisted green one. He gobbled it up and then cooed.

"Friends?" I asked.

Habanero moved his head up and down. I bent over and slowly held out my hand. Habanero rubbed the top of his head on my palm and purred.

Darcy smiled. "I think we have a dragon on our side! Habanero, do you know where the key is to unlock the cage?"

He grunted and then raced into the cottage. He

started pulling sticks and twigs out of the oven and finally came out with a round metal circle with dozens of keys on it.

Darcy and I exchanged looks as my cheeks flared with anger. "If Habanero had lit that oven, there's no way we could've gotten the key," I said. "And Hasenpfeffer would've . . ."

Darcy bit her lip. "Wow. Those two really are out for blood."

Habanero flew over to us and handed Darcy the key ring. She turned to give it to me, but I shook my head. "You can do it."

She grinned and hurried over to the cottage and placed the keys on the oven. She took out her wand and held it aloft. *"Too many choices, so little time. Show me the real key; make it mine."* An old, rusted key stood at attention, and Darcy grabbed it. She held the key up toward the cage, and a shimmering lock appeared.

"Oh, it will feel so good to get out of here," Hasenpfeffer declared. "My poor legs are cramped and I *desperately* need to go to the bathroom!"

Just as Darcy was about to fit the key into the lock, Milo stalked out of a large fragment of mirror at the edge of the woods. "Stop!" he bellowed. "You cheated, and as such you lose! I demand they be taken straight to the dungeon, and I'll skin this reptilian traitor and make boots out of his hide!"

The white cat leapt gracefully out after Milo and transformed back into the kobold, as Habanero flew off into the woods, screeching in terror.

The kobold regarded us all, shaking his head. "That's a very serious accusation," he said. "Very serious. I do not abide cheating. . . ." He looked back and forth between Darcy and me. "But I fail to see what they've done wrong."

"If that's settled, then I *really* need to go to the bathroom!" Hasenpfeffer called out.

Milo's eyes popped angrily. "'F-fail to see'?" he sputtered at the kobold. "Are you blind? They bribed that turncoat dragon into helping them. We had it all planned out, and that was *not* the way they were to complete the task."

"Give me a break!" I said, stalking over to Milo, too mad to be afraid. "There's no way we ever would've guessed where the keys were. Plus, they would've been in the middle of a fire. If we'd done it your way, Hasenpfeffer would be dead!"

Darcy cleared her throat. "Excuse me," she said calmly, folding her hands together politely. "Mr. Kobold? The task was to rescue Hasenpfeffer, correct?"

"Yes," the kobold agreed.

She swished the key in front of Milo's face. "Well, we

have the key, so we can rescue him fair and square."

Milo puffed out his chest and waved his hands wildly in the air. "But you were supposed to battle the dragon while—"

"While Hasenpfeffer roasted!" I interjected.

"Maggie," Darcy said soothingly. "Let me handle this."

I folded my arms across my chest and nodded.

"You never said the tasks had to be completed a certain way," Darcy continued, "and while you may be disappointed that we didn't zap the dragon and Hasenpfeffer didn't get roasted, we did indeed complete the task. Well, almost." She held out the key and titled her head toward the cottage. "May I?"

"Yes, of course," the kobold said as he stepped aside so she could pass.

"This is outrageous! This is a mockery of justice. This is—," Milo complained.

"Our first win," I said smugly.

Darcy unlocked the cage and lifted Hasenpfeffer out. The second she put him down, he hopped out of the cottage at top speed and disappeared into the underbrush.

Darcy raised a finger in the air and smiled sweetly at Milo. "Oh, Cousin Milo, I suggest you start preparing yourself, because you've underestimated us and you're going to be in this mirror a *very long time*."

"No hard feelings, old chap," the kobold said to Milo. "Besides, you made sure the next task is exceedingly dangerous. I suggest we let them get to it. *Milo*," he said sternly, pointing to the mirror fragment they had come from.

Milo let out an exasperated sigh. "Fine! But what about the third task?" he asked in a hushed voice. "This changes everything and gives them an unfair advantage."

"The game has begun and there's nothing to be done about that," the kobold said. "After you, then."

Just before he stepped through the mirror, Milo turned back and looked down his nose at us. "I cannot wait to see you fail miserably at your next task."

"Now, Milo," the kobold scolded, following him in, "where's your sense of sportsmanship?"

As soon as they were gone, Habanero flew out of the trees and landed on the ground in front of the basket and eagerly devoured another pepper. A minute later Hasenpfeffer hopped out of the woods, wiggling his behind.

"I feel soooo much better now. Are we ready to go home? I can't wait to show Habanero my room."

"*Our* room," I said. "But, no. We can't go just yet. We still have two more tasks to complete, and if we fail, we're *never* going home."

Hasenpfeffer chattered his teeth. "Oh, I really, really hate that kobold. I mean, just when I thought I was safe, there are more horrors to come. Tsk!" He looked up at me. "I can't believe your father would hang around with a creature that would put a rabbit's life in danger."

Habanero chirped out a series of trills and squeaks.

"Really?" Hasenpfeffer said, sitting up on his haunches. "Are you sure?"

Habanero nodded and then glanced up at Darcy and me. He warbled some more in a very agitated manner.

"I don't know," Hasenpfeffer said. "I think we really should—"

Flames shot out, scorching the ground to the right of Hasenpfeffer, who jumped a foot into the air. "Fine! Have it your way," he said testily when he landed.

"What was that all about?" I asked.

Hasenpfeffer eyed Habanero. "Nothing. He was just telling me how happy he is that I'm free."

"Happy?" Darcy said. "He almost barbecued you."

"Oh no," Hasenpfeffer said. "That's just a, uh, sign of affection."

"Can you really understand what he's saying?" I asked.

"Oh, yes. I'm very gifted that way."

I raised an eyebrow.

"All right. *All* magic rabbits have the ability to understand other creatures, but I must say I pick up new languages much quicker than the average hare."

"Can you ask Habanero where he came from?" Darcy shouted.

Hasenpfeffer rolled his eyes. "I think it's apparent he can understand you. There's no need to shout."

Habanero sat upright and waved his front claws in the air. He began a long, lilting song made of warbles and trills. Halfway through his voice deepened and became more guttural, and then the song ended with a series of mournful whines and moans.

When he was done, he hung his head, and Hasenpfeffer hopped over to him. "Poor fellow. Alone all that time. No wonder you were willing to listen to Milo. He was the first person to appear in hundreds of years, and from the sounds of it, Milo is not unlike your mistress."

My mouth dropped open. "Habanero has been in the mirror for hundreds of years?"

Hasenpfeffer looked up and nodded sadly. "His owner created this mirror. She was a powerful sorceress."

"Mr. McGuire told me about her," I said.

Hasenpfeffer sighed. "When it was time for her to die, she brought Habanero into the mirror with her, and after she passed . . ."

Habanero lifted his head into the air and howled.

A crocodile roar answered back—echoing through the forest.

Hasenpfeffer jumped. *"What was that?"*

"Ghost croc," Darcy stated matter-of-factly.

I scanned the path for any sign of Buhodu. "Let's keep going; it's not safe to stay in one place too long."

Habanero flapped his wings and rose into the air, and we started off. After we'd walked for a bit, I opened the compact. "Raphael! We completed the first task. We have Hasenpfeffer, and the dragon is now on our side."

Raphael pumped a fist in the air. "Awesome! You can do this, Maggie!"

"Is Gram there yet?"

"Yes, and Franny is using her wand to open the wall were the poppet was hidden. Look."

He held out the mirror, and I saw a bright light shooting out of the tip of Franny's wand, cutting into the wall.

Suddenly the mirror was jostled and Gram's face appeared. She looked like she'd aged ten years since this morning. "Maggie, are you all right?"

I forced a smile. "So far so good. I hope you don't mind, but Hasenpfeffer has adopted a dragon—don't worry—he's little."

Gram put a hand to her mouth to stifle a cry. "I'll never forgive myself if you can't get out of there. And what am I going to tell your parents?"

"The truth?" I said quietly. "Something I wish you'd told me earlier."

She looked away for a second and then bowed her head. "I'm sorry, Maggie. It was just so awful, I didn't want to relive it—not even for a second. When you came here, I practically held my breath and prayed you didn't have magic—prayed I wouldn't have any more heartache. But I should have told you. Maybe we could have prevented this. I hope you can forgive me."

"It's okay, Gram, but . . . I saw Grandpa. . . . Dark hair, bow tie . . ."

Tears filled her eyes. "He came back when we needed him most. He was a good man, Maggie. He just made a few mistakes. I'm so sorry; I should've told you everything."

I nodded.

"Oh, I don't know where to begin." She let out a long sigh. "As you now know, your father *is* a magician. He wasn't a happy child—he was never content hiding his magic. He was never content living a simple life. When he purchased the wooden likeness of the kobold at an estate sale, things got worse. He started casting mean-spirited spells and playing tricks on non-magical people. Your grandfather thought the kobold was encouraging him, feeding off his magic. I was not so sure."

"What do you mean, Gram?"

Gram's hand shook, and her reflection bounced around. "Your father's behavior got worse after the kobold arrived, but he was already on the path . . ." Gram put her free hand to her chest.

"The path to what?"

"The path to evil. Your grandfather couldn't see it. He was convinced the kobold was to blame, and maybe he was." She shook her head. "I don't know how, but your grandfather found a spell to block anyone from accessing your father's magic. He thought it would keep the kobold from becoming more powerful. It worked too well. After the spell took effect, your father couldn't access his own magic. He was powerless."

I put my hand to my mouth, knowing how horrible it would be to have my powers taken away.

"Your grandfather was devastated about what happened, and when he realized the spell could never be reversed, he flew into a rage and encased the kobold's poppet in a block of salt, imprisoning the creature. And then . . ." Gram sobbed. "And then he erased your father's memory of all magic. He also tampered with the memories of anyone who knew that your father had magic because he was so ashamed of what he'd done."

"That's why everyone thought magic had skipped a generation in our family," I said.

"Yes," Gram said. "But I knew, and the knowledge ate at me all these years."

"Hey, look!" Franny's voice called out.

Gram gasped, and the compact fell and clattered to the floor.

"I got it," Raphael cried. The next moment, he was holding the compact. "Whoa. You have to see this," he said. He pointed the mirror toward the wall.

"Darcy, come look!" I called out.

She leaned in. "There it is."

Inside the hole in the wall was a small, roughly carved wooden figure about seven or eight inches high. Pointed ears poked out from its head, but what really struck me was the wide open, laughing mouth. The poppet's wooden shoes remained in what was now a mostly eroded block of salt. I stared at the face and could almost hear a big belly laugh coming from the statuette, but I knew what the real kobold was like, and a jolly fellow he wasn't.

"What happened to the salt?" Darcy asked.

A large drip hit the top of the poppet, and everyone drew in a breath.

"A leak!" Gram cried. "All this trouble because of a leaky pipe!"

Franny put an arm around Gram. "Help is on the

way. I just wish I had enough power by myself to pull off the spell to trap the kobold."

Raphael put the compact up to his face. "We found the spell, but you have to be a level eighty-six to perform it. Viola Klemp has located a volunteer. She lives on Long Island, but she's on her way."

"Good! The sooner we get rid of this thing the better!"

"Maggie?" Gram called out. Raphael passed the compact to her. "About the kobold."

"I'll finish what Grandpa couldn't!"

Suddenly there was a commotion in the shop. "Where is my daughter?"

Mrs. Davenport pushed into view.

"Darcy, your mom is in the shop."

Darcy grabbed the compact from my hand. "Mommy?"

I looked over Darcy's shoulder, and Mrs. Davenport's flushed face appeared in the compact. "Baby! Are you all right?"

Darcy nodded. "Yeah, for now."

"Who is responsible for this?" she demanded. "I will personally see to it that whoever got you into this is severely punished!"

"It's Milo," Darcy said flatly.

Mrs. Davenport's eyes widened. "Cousin Milo?"

"Yes, and he refuses to help out in any way."

Mrs. Davenport jutted her chin out. "Well, guess who is off the Christmas card list!"

"Ghost croc heading our way!" Hasenpfeffer hollered.

I turned and saw the low, lumbering shape of Buhodu clomping toward us. "Let's move!" I said, pulling Darcy along the path."

"Mother, I have to go," Darcy said, looking over her shoulder. "I'll be back as soon I can, okay?"

She slammed the compact shut and gave it to me. I stuffed it into my back pocket and then scooped up Hasenpfeffer and swung him over my shoulder.

"Do crocodiles eat rabbits?" he asked with a quivering voice.

"They'll eat just about anything."

"Mirror to the right!" Darcy called out. She pointed her wand and yelled, *"Illuminate!"*

The fragment, some four feet off the path, lit up like fireworks on the Fourth of July. Buhodu veered off toward it, and we slowed to walking.

Once Buhodu disappeared into the fragment, I put Hasenpfeffer on the ground and exhaled. "I hate that croc."

"*You* hate it? Humph," Hasenpfeffer groused. "Try being the tastiest member of our party. I just know I'd be the first one to be eaten."

We continued walking in silence, and I became aware

of a number of butterflies and other insects flitting or hopping quickly down the path toward us.

Darcy swiped at her face. "Ugh! I walked into a spiderweb."

A cobweb stretched across my mouth, and I brushed it away. "Me too."

Habanero swooped down and flew along at our sides, and I could see gossamer strands trailing from his scales as he trilled happily.

"For pity's sake!" Hasenpfeffer grumbled, examining a paw. "What's all over this path?"

"That's really weird," I said, looking at streak after streak of sticky white threads crisscrossing the dirt. "Maybe a spider egg sac hatched recently?"

Hasenpfeffer looked up at me with wide, pleading eyes. "Could you carry me? It's sticking to my paws and making them itchy."

Habanero growled, and I looked up to see him sitting on a branch pulling at more webbing that was caught around his face.

"Pfff. It's all over me," Hasenpfeffer whined, spitting a web out of his mouth as I scooped him up.

"Cool," Darcy said. "Come look."

"Spiders?" I asked as I headed over to where she was standing on the edge of the path.

She shook her head. "No. It's a praying mantis. I used to have one as a pet until my mother found it and *dumped* it out into the garden." She put her nose into the air. "'Bugs are not proper pets for young ladies,'" she said, imitating her mother.

She looked away. "You probably think that's a stupid pet."

"Are you forgetting that my parents are entomologists? Insects were the only kind of pet I was allowed to have. We had hissing cockroaches, walking sticks, crickets, and an ever changing assortment of moths and butterflies at my house. It didn't make me very popular at school."

"Sorry I called you Bug Girl that first day of class. I actually like insects. They're like aliens right here on earth." She turned to me with a sly smile on her face. "Didn't you say Milo was afraid of insects?"

"Yes."

She scrunched up her freckled nose in thought and clucked her tongue like Mr. McGuire always does. My shoulders slumped. We still needed to rescue him and Fiona, and Milo had warned us the tasks would just get harder.

"Here's what I'm thinking," Darcy said. "Do you have

any of the magic food from the spell you used on the mice in Scotland?"

Hasenpfeffer groaned and buried his head on my shoulder. "Don't mention Scotland!"

"Yeah. We didn't use it all."

"If you can get some of the food, I have an idea about how to let Milo know that he picked the wrong two girls to mess with!"

"I studied up on retrieval spells when we were researching a way to find the selkie skins—"

Hasenpfeffer moaned. *"Stop talking about the trip to Scotland. I almost died!"*

"Sorry." I patted him on the back. "Anyway," I said to Darcy, "I'm not sure it'll work with us being in the mirror, but I'll give it a try."

I juggled Hasenpfeffer with one arm and took my wand out. I pictured the jar that contained the ingredients to control animals. "Middle shelf, between the jar of crow feathers and the canister of origin powder," I said quietly to myself. I pointed my wand at the path. Concentrating on the image in my head, I closed my eyes. *"In my mind I take a peek, see the image that I seek. It's too far so I beseech, bring it now within my reach."*

I opened my eyes and smiled. On the path right in

front of me sat a small container of animal-control feed, something lion tamers use to make creatures obey their every command. "Here you go," I said, handing it to Darcy.

She smirked as she held the jar up and examined the contents. "I cannot wait for Milo to meet the newest member of our team."

9

A Sticky Situation

She opened the jar and then, to my surprise, caught a small cricket that had joined the increasing number of insects in the vicinity. I stepped closer as she dipped the cricket into the jar, coating it with the magic food.

I grimaced. "You're not—are you?"

She nodded. "Circle of life." She then dangled the cricket by one leg in front of the mantis. The large green insect's forearms reached out and snatched the cricket with lightning speed. The next second the mantis began eagerly devouring the poor creature, crunching noisily as she threw the cricket's wings aside.

"Horrible!" Hasenpfeffer squealed.

Darcy rolled her eyes. "I'm sure parsley feels the same way when you eat it."

He gasped. "Do you really think so?"

She narrowed her eyes. "You never know. The leaves could be screaming on the inside." She winked at me.

"Oh," Hasenpfeffer moaned. "I just know I'll be haunted by wailing parsley in my sleep tonight—if I'm even still alive by bedtime."

When the mantis finished her meal, Darcy held her wand over the insect and recited the little-known spell that Gammy Davenport had used years before to magically train squirrels for a traveling show. *Wild beasts big and small, obey my beck and heed my call. Complete the task; do not fail. Let only my will prevail.*

The mantis cocked her triangular head and gazed up at Darcy with her oversize eyes. Darcy held out her palm. "Marilla, come!"

The mantis walked onto Darcy's palm with her spindly back legs. Darcy beamed and held Marilla up to her face. "Isn't she beautiful?"

"Yeah, but 'Marilla'?" I asked.

Darcy held the mantis up to me. "She looks like a

Marilla, don't you think? Tough on the outside—"

"Looks more like a Vlad the Impaler, if you ask me," Hasenpfeffer muttered.

"And sweet on the inside?" I asked, talking over my rabbit. "Like Marilla from *Anne of Green Gables*, right?

Darcy smiled. "Exactly."

"I've read some of those books too," I said. "But do you really think one little mantis is going to scare Milo?"

"Oh, I'm not finished yet." Darcy used her shoe to push aside some of the sticky threads on the path, and then she put Marilla down. "Gammy does this trick at holiday parties after she's had too much champagne. It drives my mother crazy." She looked over her shoulder at Hasenpfeffer and me. "You might want to step back a bit."

"I don't think I'm going to like this," Hasenpfeffer whispered into my ear. "No, I *know* I'm not going to like it!"

Darcy pointed her wand at Marilla. *"Tom Thumb and tiny ants, reach for things they know they can't. Like a tree stretches to the sun, fulfill my wish when the spell is done."*

Instantly, Marilla shot up until she was almost seven feet tall. Her mandibles clicked and clacked loudly as she waved her huge spiked forearms in the air, shredding the cobwebs hanging in her way.

I gulped. "Do you really think this is a good idea? What if she gets hungry? A little cricket won't be very satisfying."

"We'll feed the rabbit to her."

Hasenpfeffer bolted upright in my arms.

"Just kidding," Darcy said.

Hasenpfeffer chattered angrily. "That was in very poor taste! And I can't believe *anyone* would find making giant insects at holiday parties at all festive!"

Darcy rolled her eyes. "Gammy doesn't super-size insects; she supersizes hors d'oeuvres. You know, like pigs in a blanket and stuffed mushrooms? There is something inherently funny about a giant pastry-wrapped hot dog. Well, to everyone but my mother, that is."

"Humph." Hasenpfeffer sniffed indignantly. "If you wanted to supersize parsley, I'd be all for it. Mmm," Hasenpfeffer said dreamily.

I eyed Marilla warily. "Are you sure you can control her?"

"Marilla, shake hands!" Darcy commanded.

Darcy held out her hand, and the mantis slowly extended one gigantic claw. It dwarfed Darcy's hand as she shook it.

"Marilla, roll over!"

The mantis flung herself onto the ground and rolled, kicking up a cloud of dust in the dry earth.

I laughed. "That is something I never thought I'd see. Darcy, it's official. You are the Master of Mantises!" I said, trying my best to sound like Milo.

She laughed, and Hasenpfeffer shook his head. "I fail to see what's so funny about mutant insects. Must be a preteen girl thing, but as I'd like to go home, can we move on to the next task?"

A warm breeze blew down the path, carrying more silk threads that stuck to us as they caught on our faces and arms. "Eh," I said, brushing them off quickly. "Yeah, let's get going."

"Should I magic a saddle for old Marilla?" Darcy asked as we started walking. "We could ride into town in style."

I stared at her for a second, and then we both burst out laughing again. "You're one of a kind, Darcy."

As we continued into the forest, the webbing in the trees and the strands floating in the air got thicker and thicker. Habanero struggled to fly, and then finally gave up and walked alongside us—weaving in and out between our legs. Every once in a while he'd shoot Marilla a nervous look accompanied by a high-pitched whine.

Soon thick sheets of silk draped across the path, and Darcy had Marilla cut through them with her spiked forearms.

I saw the white cat up ahead. It turned and regarded us and then zipped down a fork in the path leading to the right.

"We must be getting close." I said. "Are you thinking what I'm thinking?" I asked after we passed through an opening.

Darcy rolled her eyes. "Duh. Spiders."

"Yeah," I said. "We're definitely in for some sort of arachnid encounter."

Darcy held out her hand and tugged on a thick string. "And from the size of these strands, I'm thinking *big* ones."

Hasenpfeffer groaned yet again. "Just think about giant parsley and not giant spiders," he whispered to himself. "Giant parsley, giant parsley, giant parsley."

We pushed through yet another sheet of webbing, and when we came out on the other side, there was a tall web-covered tower made of dark red bricks. Thousands of strands of silk glistened like spun sugar from the single turret as the strands stretched down to the ground and to the surrounding trees. The only thing that wasn't covered in webbing was the huge red flag bearing Milo's face atop the turret.

There was a solitary window some eighty feet up, and a lone figure sat motionless, gazing out. The person had a thick braid made of cobwebs instead of hair, that hung down to the ground.

I looked up at the castle and whistled, wondering when the web makers would appear. "Someone obviously has a thing for fairy tales—with a nasty twist."

"Do you hear that?" Darcy asked, pointing toward the window.

I leaned forward, cocked my ear toward the tower, and heard faint, muffled screams. "That's *Fiona!* They have her wrapped up like a mummy! I'm guessing they've replaced the witch again—with spiders this time."

Darcy scoffed. "What's next, *Beauty and the Beast*, with Mr. McGuire playing the part of Beauty and a T. rex playing the beast?"

"That's not funny," I snapped. "Fiona will be spider chow if we don't rescue her."

Darcy nodded in agreement and then looked up at the tower with pinched a face. "Looking around at the abundance of webs everywhere, I think it's safe to say we could *all* be spider chow." She looked at me and bit her lip. "Fiona could really be in trouble—us, too. I knew Milo was not the nicest guy, but I never thought he was this evil."

"Some people are just really good at covering up

what's inside, and maybe the kobold has brought out the worst in him."

Darcy pushed up her sleeves and held her wand high. "Well, what are we waiting for? It's time we kicked some eight-legged butt!"

"I don't like spiders," Hasenpfeffer sobbed as he buried his head in my armpit. "Not even those daddy longlegs that are supposed to be harmless. Nothing with spidery legs like that is harmless."

I knew it was going to be awkward battling spiders while holding a panicky Hasenpfeffer, but I also knew it wasn't safe to put him down where he'd be an easy target. I spied a mirror fragment and got an idea.

"Hasenpfeffer, do you want to hide in a mirror so you can stay out of the battle?"

He poked his head out from under my arm. "Oh, yes! Anywhere but here!" he said, looking around in wide-eyed terror.

I looked at a piece of mirror the size of a file cabinet leaning on a tree close by. "Milo and the kobold have been traveling in them—Buhodu, too—so I'm thinking they're safe to go into. I'll take you in and make sure no one can get to you."

Hasenpfeffer craned his neck toward the mirror. "Sounds good to me!" he squeaked.

"Darcy, let me get Hasenpfeffer somewhere safe, and then we'll tackle Castle Cobweb."

She let out an exasperated sigh. "If you ask me, the rabbit isn't pulling his weight. He's got teeth and claws. He could inflict some damage." She held two fingers up to her mouth like oversize rabbit incisors and made some chattering noise.

I cradled Hasenpfeffer in my arms and shook my head. "Cut him some slack. He weighs ten pounds—"

"Twelve, actually—perfectly normal for my breed!" Hasenpfeffer stated.

"And," I continued, "he's still recovering from the shape-shifter bite—and he almost got roasted today."

Darcy put a hand on Marilla's long emerald green neck. "Fine. Marilla here can pick up the slack."

"Okay. I'll try to hurry, but if something should attack, just yell for me and I'll be right out!"

"Don't worry; if I'm attacked, you'll be the first to know about it," Darcy said flatly.

I readjusted Hasenpfeffer in my arms and quickly walked to the mirror fragment. I bent down on my knees and brushed the webs away. "How does it work, do you think?" I said aloud. "Do you just walk in?"

"Actually," Hasenpfeffer said, "that dreadful kobold said that if you have enough magic, you can travel through the mirrors. I heard him and Milo arguing. Milo was boasting about being the Master of Mirrors, but the kobold kept insisting that it was only because of his help that Milo could move about the realms."

"Well, I'm more powerful than Milo, but that kobold definitely has me beat. Let's give it a try, though."

I reached my free hand out, and it effortlessly cut the plane of the mirror. Habanero whined and brushed his head against my arm. "You stay here; we're going to need your help, okay?"

Habanero let out a mournful sigh.

"Don't worry. I'll make sure Hasenpfeffer will be safe."

Habanero nodded and then walked dejectedly back over to Darcy.

"Here goes nothing." I ducked down and scrambled into the fragment. Once inside, I saw there were dozens of other mirrors hovering just above the ground, like echoes, but they each seemed to have their own distinct shimmer. The air around was gray and misty, reminding me of my first trip into the mirror, when Mr. McGuire told me it wasn't wise to stay in one place.

"What looks good?" I asked hurriedly, hoping Hasenpfeffer's animal instincts would lead us in the right direction and I could get back to Fiona quickly.

He sniffed the air and then finally pointed his paw.

"That one, with the soft green light. It reminds me of parsley with the sun shining on it."

I headed for the greenish mirror, and when we stepped through, I gasped. My feet touched down on a path of polished white stones that led to a small but magnificently carved pagoda sitting in a valley surrounded by lush fog-capped mountains. Dragon statues resembling Habanero stood erect guarding the door, and a clear brook splashed noisily through beautiful gardens of twisted bonsai trees, ponds, and wooden bridges.

Hasenpfeffer chattered happily. "Oh, this is the perfect place to hide! Have I mentioned that Milo and I were very big in Asia?"

"Once or twice," I muttered.

I carried him up the steps to the front door and knocked—with my wand ready. When no one replied, I turned the doorknob and went in. The pagoda was one large room with a person lying on her back atop a large marble base. My heart raced, but then I saw it was a statue carved in jade. I walked up to see that it looked like a Chinese woman; her eyes were closed as though she was sleeping. The statue was dressed in a high-necked blue silk dress, and a wooden wand was clutched in her stone hand. My eyes traced the dress, and I realized it was the same embroidered fabric that covered the magic mirror in the repair shop.

"This must be some sort of memorial for the creator of the mirror." I wondered if seeing it would have made Habanero happy or sad. He may very well have been living here before the kobold started mucking with the mirror's realms.

I put Hasenpfeffer down and looked out the back windows. There weren't any other houses or any signs of anyone living. "I think you'll have the place to yourself," I said. "You'll be safe here."

Hasenpfeffer sat on his haunches and surveyed the room. "This is certainly a nice change of pace." He sighed. "But I guess you need to go so you can get Fiona," he said softly.

"I'll be back as soon as I can, and I'll leave the door open so you can enjoy the gardens."

I headed for the door, and Hasenpfeffer hopped over to me. "Maggie? You are coming back, aren't you?"

I turned to him and forced a smile to my face. "Yes, of course," I said, trying to sound more confident than I felt.

Before I left the mirror shard, I took one last look at Hasenpfeffer, who was sitting on an arched bridge, peering into a pond filled with brightly colored koi. I took comfort in the fact that if I didn't come back, Hasenpfeffer would finally get to "retire" in Asia like he used to dream about.

I exited the mirror and saw Marilla standing at attention, her bulbous head jerking around, scanning the area.

"Anything?" I asked Darcy in a hushed voice.

"It's been quiet—too quiet," she replied.

We both got our wands out and slowly walked toward the tower.

"I haven't seen even one spider," Darcy whispered. "It's so weird. I mean, the webs are everywhere. Where are the spiders?"

As if on cue a black spider the size of a dinner plate dropped down in front of us from the trees. Black fangs clacked, and its shiny, humped abdomen bore the red hourglass markings of a black widow spider. My heart leapt, and as I struggled to catch my breath, I saw my terrified face reflected in its soulless black eyes. A scream finally left my mouth as the spider hit the ground and scuttled toward us.

10
Frenemies

Darcy yelled to Marilla, and in a flash the mantis had the creature firmly grasped in her spiky forearms and was happily munching on the top of its head.

"Ew!" I said, shaking my hands in the air.

Gooey green insides dripped from her mandibles, and I shuddered as bile rose in my throat.

"Good girl, Marilla!" Darcy said.

Habanero trilled excitedly. "You want in on the action?" Darcy asked.

I turned to see the dragon fly in an excited swirl in front of Darcy. "You'll get a pepper for every spider you take out."

I gave Darcy a weak smile. "Good idea. I'll double that offer, Habanero. Flame on!"

Suddenly dozens upon dozens of spiders poured out of the tower window and jumped down the sides to the ground on silk cords. Habanero zipped toward them like a lightning bolt, a stream of fire leading the way.

"Marilla!" Darcy commanded. "Kill the spiders, but don't stop to eat them, or they'll get you."

Marilla bowed her head and lumbered forward, waving her forearms in the air. As the spiders rushed toward us, Habanero let loose another volley of flames. Arachnids sizzled and popped like firecrackers, sending cooked spider guts bursting into the air. Marilla crushed the fiends with her giant claws, but it was clear she'd be overwhelmed soon.

Darcy and I shot out bolts of magic from our wands, and spiders exploded with satisfying bangs. "There are too many of them," Darcy called out. "We need to think of a spell—" Darcy's eyes widened, and I turned toward the tower.

The webbing around the tower had caught fire.

"Oh no!" I cried. "It's going up in flames. We have to get to Fiona!" I surveyed the scene as my mind raced. *"I wish I was in the tower!"*

I braced myself for the magic to whisk me away, but nothing happened. *"I wish I was in the tower!"* I shrieked again.

"You *can't* transport yourself, remember?" Darcy yelled as she shot jolts of magic toward the encroaching horde.

My heart skipped a beat as I saw the cobweb braid acting like a fuse, rapidly sending flaming sparks toward Fiona. "Habanero!" I yelled. "I need you!"

The dragon turned on a dime and flapped his wings toward me. "Take me to the window," I shouted.

He swooped down, and I latched onto his hind claws. He pumped his wings, and we rose just a foot from the ground. "I'm too heavy!" I yelled, watching the fire soar up the cobweb braid toward the window.

Darcy pointed her wand at Habanero. *"Tom Thumb and tiny ants, reach for things they know they can't. Like a tree stretches to the sun, fulfill my wish when the spell is done."*

In a flash Habanero grew before my eyes. He flapped his new ten-foot wings and effortlessly brought me to the tower window. I threw myself in and started tearing through the webbing surrounding Fiona.

When her mouth was uncovered, Fiona sobbed. "Maggie, thank goodness you're here!"

I tore at the silk wrapping around her. "I'm going to get you out of here!"

Smoke filled the air, and I realized Habanero's wings were fanning the flames. I looked out the window and saw that Darcy and Marilla were severely outnumbered.

Fiona was as white as a ghost, and her eyes were filled with terror as I frantically yanked more silk away from her. "I was so scared, and now—"

"No time to talk, Fiona!" I pulled away the last bit around her ankles, and she was free.

"Maggie!" Darcy screamed. *"A little help, please?"*

"Fiona, we have to go!" I took her hand and pulled her toward the window.

"I just want to go home. I don't want to see any more spiders," she sobbed.

"I want that too, but right now we have to get out of this tower!"

I leaned out the window and cupped my hands around my mouth. The heat from the flames was almost unbearable. "Habanero!" I yelled.

Habanero soared up to the window, kicking up flames and ash. I jumped onto Habanero's back and positioned myself between the great spikes running along his spine.

I turned and motioned for Fiona to follow me. "Get on!"

Her tangled hair flew around her face as she shook her head. "I'm scared!" she said with a quaking voice.

Flames were licking the windowsill, and I choked on the smoke. Darcy was busy zapping spiders, but it was obvious she couldn't get them all and she'd be completely surrounded any second. "There's no time to be scared! We have to help Darcy—now! Jump!"

Fiona's lower lip quivered.

"Maggie! Where are you?" Darcy called out.

I looked down, and webbing was drifting everywhere in the smoky air. "*Come on*, Fiona! You have to do it."

Fiona shook her head. "I can't!"

"Keep it steady, Habanero," I said. "Take my hand, Fiona!" I held out my hand, but Fiona just shook her head. "C'mon!" I cried. "We don't have much time!" Finally she grabbed hold, and I pulled her toward me. With a scream she landed unsteadily on the dragon's back and started to slide down Habanero's side.

"No, you don't!" I grabbed on to a spike for leverage and then yanked Fiona back up.

"Hold on tight," I said, and she wrapped her arms around my waist. "Get Darcy, Habanero!" I commanded.

Habanero trilled and then folded his wings back and dropped to the ground like a stone.

"Darcy!" I yelled as Fiona screamed. "We're coming for you!"

Darcy looked up, covered in webbing. She lobbed a series of blasts at the spiders and then held her hands up. Habanero latched on to her and lifted her off the ground. "Marilla!" she cried. "Fly away!"

The mantis flapped her large green wings and tried to lift off the ground. She struggled and flapped some more but was too heavy. Silk strands filled the air around her, tangling her legs and wings, and then tears filled my eyes as Marilla was overtaken by the eight-legged monsters.

"Get 'em, Habanero," I said through clenched teeth. "Get every last one of those stinking spiders!"

He roared and flapped his wings, blowing all the spiders off Marilla. The mantis lay on her side unmoving, and I could hear Darcy cry out. Habanero expelled a mighty blast of fire at the crowd of spiders who were scrambling over one another to get back to where Marilla lay. They burst into flames, and I cheered as Habanero soared up and away from the scene.

I turned back to see the flag bearing Milo's face catch fire, but it gave me no satisfaction. We still had one more of Milo's tasks to face.

With a few flaps of Habanero's wings, we cleared the area. From up high I could fully see the maze of mirrors the kobold had assembled, with a castle in the middle. Habanero glided low to the ground and found a clearing to land in. Darcy jumped down, and Habanero skittered to a stop beside her.

Darcy looked up, her face streaked with soot and tears. "I never should've brought her along," she said bitterly. "If I'd just left her alone, she'd still be alive."

"Someone died?" Fiona asked in a whisper.

"It was sort of a pet that Darcy found. The spiders got it."

Fiona gasped. "Oh, that's horrible."

We slid off Habanero's back, and Fiona hugged me. "Thanks for saving me. I was so scared being wrapped up in that room with wall-to-wall spiders. They kept staring at me and waving their pincers around, and I kept thinking—"

"I know." I hugged her back and saw Darcy glancing sideways at us.

Fiona walked over to Darcy. "You, too. Thanks." She held out her arms, and Darcy took a step forward, but then hesitated. Fiona went up to meet her and gave Darcy a hug. Darcy stiffened. "Sorry about your friend," Fiona said gently.

Darcy exhaled and put her head on Fiona's shoulder. She hugged Fiona briefly and then took a step back. "It's okay," she said, wiping a tear from her eye. "It was just a bug."

I looked her in the eye, and it was obvious Marilla had been more than just a bug to Darcy.

"So," Fiona said, eyeing Habanero, her eyes as round as saucers. "I see you've acquired a dragon. I'm assuming he's tame."

I nodded. "Yes, and he's recently had a growth spurt." I turned to Darcy. "That was quick thinking."

Darcy nodded, a slight smile coming to her lips.

I held out a hand to Habanero. "Habanero, this is Fiona. Fiona—Habanero."

Fiona bowed to the dragon. "It's very nice to meet you, Habanero. Thank you for rescuing me from that tower."

Habanero bowed his head and then trilled happily.

"This has been quite a day," Fiona said, pulling cobwebs from her matted hair. "I've been dragged into a magic mirror by malicious vines, wrapped like a mummy in sticky webbing, and locked in a doorless tower with a hundred or so mutant spiders. The only good thing is that I've just ridden my very first dragon, but I think I'm ready to go home now."

I grimaced. "We can't go yet. We still have one more task to complete, and if we don't complete it—"

"We *will* complete it," Darcy said with narrowed eyes. She brushed her tangled frizzy hair behind her ears with determination. "And you were right, Maggie. I do like to be number one. No, I *need* to be number one, so there is *no way* I'm going to let that crazy cousin of mine keep us in this mirror one second longer than necessary. Milo the Magnificent is going down!"

Suddenly, Hasenpfeffer bounded out of a nearby mirror fragment as if something was chasing him.

"Are you okay?" I asked.

He looked over his shoulder at the fragment. "Yes, but I couldn't shake the feeling I was being watched. My fur was literally standing on end, so I left to find you."

"How did you know where to come out?" I asked.

"I heard you talking. Oh! While I was figuring out which mirror to exit from, I heard the kobold and Milo arguing. Let's just say, that bromance is not as happy as they'd like us to think."

I looked at the shard. "What were they arguing about?"

"I didn't stay too long to listen, but something about Mr. McGuire."

My eyes widened. "Maybe I can eavesdrop and get some info on the last task! Wait here. I'll be back soon."

"Are you sure I'll be safe with . . ." He cocked his head at Darcy, who rolled her eyes.

"Yes. I wouldn't leave you if I didn't think you'd be safe," I said soothingly.

Darcy wrinkled her nose at Hasenpfeffer, but she was smiling when she did it.

"Be careful," Fiona said, scooping Hasenpfeffer up into her arms.

"You too."

I walked into the mirror fragment and shivered in the cold, misty fog. The mirrors hovered and shimmered, and I cocked my head, trying to figure out which mirror would lead me to the kobold and Milo.

"They have an unfair advantage!" I heard Milo yelling, and I walked toward a mirror with a shimmering red glow.

"But they don't know that," the kobold replied.

My heart pounding, I crept inside and slipped behind some velvet curtains. I peeked out to see that Milo and the kobold were in what looked like a throne room. Milo sat on an enormous chair with plush red velvet cushions. The chair sat in the middle of a raised pink-tinged marble platform. Tapestries adorned the walls, with images of Milo performing tricks woven into the silken threads. The kobold was sitting on a small three-legged stool at the bottom of the platform, with an open book in his lap. More mirror fragments lined the walls, and I figured these were the ones the two were traveling through.

"But what if they figure it out?" Milo continued.

The kobold looked up from the book. "Well, then you lose and I set them free."

Milo stalked down the platform steps and started to pace back and forth. "Why did you have to set up this bargain to begin with?" He pounded his fist into his palm. "If I lose because of your silly troll rules, I'll—"

The kobold jumped up from the stool, and Milo recoiled.

"I'm not a troll!" the kobold snapped, pointing a finger angrily at Milo. "Take it back or else!"

"I'm *s-sorry* my little friend," Milo stammered. He pulled on the sides of his long handlebar mustache. "My temper sometimes gets the best of me." He stared, wide eyed, at the kobold, who stood with his hands curled into fists at his hips.

"You'd *best* keep it under control, or I will take this castle down with a snap of my fingers and you can find yourself a tree stump for a throne!"

"Now, now, dear friend," Milo cooed. "Don't you worry your little head for another second!" He smiled sweetly. "I shall be as good as gold. You can trust me, and soon we shall have our revenge on the Malloys for what they have put us through.

"Oh, and you have suffered the most, dear friend. Why, it breaks my heart to think of the torture you endured." Milo sniffed and pulled out a white handkerchief from his suit pocket. He dabbed crocodile tears, and I shook my head in disgust.

The kobold nodded and sat back down. He sighed. "I had such hopes for the girl. She seemed the opposite of her father. . . . Tsk."

"Oh, she has a black heart for sure. To send me into the mirror like she did—knowing there was no escape, no hope. Well, until you came along and lifted my spirits like the true friend you are."

My face twisted in anger, and it was all I could do to remain hidden and not jump out and call Milo a liar.

The kobold smiled. "It really was quite lucky for you that I found my way into the mirror, or you may very well have been trapped indefinitely—like I would have been trapped in the block of salt, if not for a fortuitous leak!"

"Yes, it was most fortunate, and I am forever in your debt." Milo put a hand to his chest. "If I may ask you again if you might reconsider—"

"No!" The kobold said. "I cannot set you free. We have to see this through." He got up and rested his book on the stool. He walked to an ornate table and stood on his toes to reach for the parchment scroll. "I cannot alter the agreement, and it's unlikely they will be able to complete the third task."

Milo rolled his eyes and marched back up to his throne. "It was unlikely they would complete the first two tasks—yet they did!"

"I am a bit surprised," the kobold stated, "but perhaps we underestimated those girls."

Milo scowled. *"Those girls!* All my lovely spiders destroyed, and the dragon! I cannot believe they have the dragon! Oh, that traitorous reptile. I could wring his skinny little neck. I could dine on dragon steaks. I could—"

"Temper!" the kobold cautioned.

Milo took in a deep breath and then exhaled slowly. He smiled again, but it was obvious it was difficult to do so. "Given the time element of the third task, they are bound to fail, and we shall have our revenge—and I will be free."

The kobold nodded, but I couldn't help but think he looked disappointed. "Yes," he said softly. "It is highly unlikely they would be able to complete the final task *without* the time limit. As it is, it's next to impossible."

I dashed out from behind the curtains and back into no-man's-land. I heard Hasenpfeffer wailing and raced to the mirror fragment, thinking, *What now?*

11

True Love's Kiss

I exited the fragment to find Buhodu bellowing at Darcy and Fiona, who were sitting in the branches of a tree. Hasenpfeffer was huddled in Fiona's lap, and Habanero was hovering over the crocodile, who snapped at the peppery flames Habanero was shooting out.

"Are you *sure* ghost crocodiles can't climb trees?" Hasenpfeffer was yelling hysterically. Fiona shifted on the branch, and Hasenpfeffer wailed. "Don't let me fall! He'd eat me in one snap of his horrible jaws."

"I'm *not* going to let you fall," Fiona said.

"And I told you already a hundred times, he's not

coming up, and even if he did, we could have Habanero take us away," Darcy replied irritably. "Now keep it down. You're giving me a headache."

"But what about Maggie?" he asked. "We couldn't leave her."

Darcy shook her head. "We could circle around until she comes out."

"If only you hadn't dropped your wand," Hasenpfeffer complained. "Then you could've gotten rid of that beast."

"Sorry," Darcy said, "but that croc came out of nowhere and startled me!"

"I'm back!" I called.

"Thank goodness," Darcy said. "The rabbit is driving me crazy."

Buhodu turned to me and roared.

"Yeah, yeah!" I said. "Same to you!" I threw a spell at the mirror fragment I'd just come out of and squinted as it lit up like a bonfire. Buhodu charged toward the light, and I ducked around the back of the glass. "Please let him go in," I whispered to myself.

"All clear," Fiona said after a few seconds.

I walked back around and shook my head. "I hope the next mirror he goes into is the one Milo and that creepy little kobold are in! They've got something bad planned, and we need to get moving fast. The final task has a *time limit* to it."

"Time limit?" Darcy said as she jumped down from the branch. She picked her wand up off the ground. "No one said anything about a time limit when we got suckered into this mess."

"I think the limit is Milo's 'special touch' and his way of ensuring we fail." I looked at Darcy and Fiona. "But we won't!"

Fiona smiled hopefully as she hopped down with Hasenpfeffer in her arms. "Right."

"Let's fly above the walls of the maze and see if we can figure out where the final task is. It'll be quicker than walking." Habanero landed on the ground, and we all climbed up onto his back. "Let's go, boy," I said.

The dragon shot into the sky, and I scanned the maze. "Do you see anything?"

Fiona pointed down. "There's a castle in the middle."

"I don't think it's there," I replied.

"There's the stupid white cat," Darcy said bitterly, pointing ahead. "Should I try to zap it?"

The kobold in cat form was trotting down a path below, a short distance from the castle. "As tempting as that is, I don't think it's a good idea." The cat made a right turn at one split, and then a quick left. I looked ahead at the path it was traveling on and saw what looked like a large canopy bed placed in a dead-end corner of the maze. "There! Do you see that bed, Habanero? Land there."

Habanero craned his neck and then zipped down to where I was pointing.

"*Sleeping Beauty?*" Darcy asked with a shrug. "How are they going to work Mr. McGuire into that story?"

"We'll find out soon enough. Get your wand ready. Who knows what they'll have guarding the bed."

Habanero hit the ground running and as he slowed to a stop, I saw the white cat leap into a mirror lining the maze wall. I jumped off Habanero's back and ran toward the bed. My heart thumped hard in my chest when I saw it was Mr. McGuire lying motionless on the plush bed with red velvet covers. His eyes were closed and his hands were folded across his chest as if he were lying in a casket.

Fiona gasped as she approached. "Is he okay?"

With a shaky hand I reached out and touched Mr. McGuire's wrist. Tears flooded my eyes as I felt a faint pulse. "He's alive."

"Thank goodness," she said breathlessly.

Darcy came over and took Mr. McGuire's glasses out of her pocket and placed them gently on the bridge of his nose. "He'll need these when he wakes up." She then scanned the area with her wand raised. "What do we do?"

I turned around and examined the dead end with my heart pounding, expecting something to come rushing down the path at us. "I don't know. I thought we'd have to fight something, but so far there's nothing." I walked around the mirrored dead end, my puzzled expression reflected in the glass. "Milo made it sound like this was going to be really difficult."

"Hey, what's this?" Fiona asked. She leaned over the bed and pulled a round pocket watch with a fancy *M* engraved on it out of Mr. McGuire's shirt pocket. "Do you recognize this?" she asked me.

I shook my head. "No, but I have a feeling that *M* stands for Milo and not McGuire." I took the watch and opened it. Inside, a digital readout was running backward. "This is the timer. We have thirty minutes until it runs down."

Fiona frowned. "That doesn't give us a lot of time to figure this out. Um, Sleeping Beauty woke up from a kiss from Prince Charming, right? You know, true love's first kiss. So I'm thinking someone has to kiss him and he'll wake up."

Darcy looked at me expectantly. "So who do we get to kiss him so we can get out of here?"

I shook my head. "I—I don't know. He's never been

married, and he's never talked about a special someone. Maybe Gram knows."

"Could it *be* your grandmother?" Fiona asked hopefully.

"Ha!" Hasenpfeffer laughed. "She's the last person I'd want kissing me."

I glared at him.

"Sorry," he said. "I guess that comment wasn't very appropriate, given the situation."

"No," I said to Hasenpfeffer, "it wasn't. But I don't think Gram is Mr. McGuire's 'true love.' And if we don't figure this out in"—I looked at the watch—"twenty-seven minutes, we'll all be living out the rest of our lives in the dungeon!"

"Well, talk to your grandmother through the compact," Darcy said. "She's our best chance for figuring this out. And when she tells us, you can try a retrieval spell to bring the person into the mirror."

I nodded and took the compact out of my back pocket. I opened it up to see Raphael's worried face. *"Where have you been?"* he shouted. "We've been worried sick." He cocked his head. "What's wrong with your hair?"

I rolled my eyes and pulled cobwebs from my hair. "I had an arachnid makeover. Long story, but sorry I've been out of touch. It's been a little crazy."

"Well, we have a full house over here." He held the

mirror out, and I could see the pinched birdlike face of Viola Klemp examining the magic mirror with some other people. Franny, Gram, and a tall dark-skinned woman were leaning over the kobold's wooden poppet on the counter. Raphael came back into view. "That lady with Franny and your grandmother is the one who will cast the spell to trap the kobold again. And guess what? They've figured out a way to make it permanent. Nothing will be able to penetrate the prison this time—not even a hurricane!"

"What are they waiting for?" I asked.

Raphael frowned. "Because it has to do with fairy magic, they have to cast the spell under a moonlit sky. Sundown is in"—he looked at his watch—"sixty-eight minutes, so it won't be long."

"No! You don't understand," I yelled. "We don't have that long. Our last task has a time limit, and it's rapidly running out. Just have them trap it like my grandfather did."

Raphael's eyes widened. "They can't. The ingredients for the spell are really rare, and they've already used them all up to make the potion. It has to be after dark."

"Get Gram. She's the only one who can help us now."

"Mrs. Malloy, Maggie needs you!" he hollered. He rushed over to the counter and gave the compact to Gram.

"Gram, who is Mr. McGuire's true love?"

"What?"

"Mr. McGuire's true love! All the tasks are fairy-tale themed, and we need Mr. McGuire's true love to kiss him—like, now—or we lose!"

Gram tapped her lip with her fingers. "I don't know. He was engaged to be married, but his fiancée had an unfortunate accident and died. He never dated anyone else."

My heart sank. "There *must* be someone else. The kobold wouldn't have set up a task that was impossible to solve, and we're running out of time."

"Oh, Maggie," Gram said. "My mind is blank."

I looked up at Mr. McGuire sleeping on the velvet bed. "Then, we're doomed."

"No, Maggie, there must be another way. There has to be!"

Tears gathered in my eyes. "I—I don't know what else to do. I just want to get out of here."

"Maggie!" Gram said firmly. "You will figure this out! Whatever you do, don't give up!"

I bit my lip and nodded, but all I wanted to do was curl up into a ball and cry. "Well, I'll keep the compact open. If you think of something, let me know."

A big tear ran down Gram's cheek. "I will."

My shoulders slumped as I looked at Darcy and Fiona. "She doesn't know."

Fiona looked away, and I knew she was trying to hide her own tears.

Darcy stomped over to me. "Have her go to Mr. McGuire's apartment. Maybe there's something in there."

"There's not enough time."

Darcy's eyes blazed with determination. "Then, you go!"

"How?"

"The same way Milo got into your apartment— through the mirrors."

I nodded and brushed away some tears. "Yes! If I could find my way to Mr. McGuire's, I could look into his apartment through the mirrors. Maybe I could spot something."

Darcy pushed me toward the mirrored walls. "Get going. We don't have any time to lose!"

I handed her the compact. "Keep in touch with Gram. Maybe she'll think of something."

I raced into the nearest fragment and spun around in the misty gloom. "Which mirror?" I muttered to myself.

I caught a glimpse of a white tail swishing in the distant fog. "The kobold," I whispered. The wheels in my head turned. The cat had always appeared before each task as if it was leading us in the right direction. I thought about how Gram had said she wasn't entirely convinced the kobold was to blame for all of my father's problems. And the kobold had told me he'd been trying to help Dad. He also tried to talk to me before Milo butted in and sent Habanero after Hasenpfeffer.

Was it possible my grandfather had been wrong about the kobold—that he was really innocent? What if the kobold had been trying to help me all along? But why?

I rushed forward into the mist where I'd seen the cat's tail. A fragment floating nearby shimmered with a yellow mist. I stepped inside, and there was nothing but an empty room with white walls. Four small mirrors were hanging on different walls, and each mirror was a different shape and size.

The nearest mirror was set in a cabinet, like you'd see in a bathroom. I walked over and looked into it to see a small bathroom. A razor and shaving cream were on the sink, and my heart leapt when I saw a pair of suspenders hanging on a hook on the wall. I was looking into Mr. McGuire's bathroom!

I scanned the bathroom, but there were no clues as to Mr. McGuire's true love.

I walked over to the next mirror. It was plain with

a simple wood border. I looked in and saw it was his bedroom. A single bed, neatly made, stood in a corner. Bookshelves lined the walls, crammed with books and knickknacks. A pair of pajamas sat folded on a chest at the foot of the bed, and there was an open book on a bedside table. I balled my hands into fists and shook them impatiently.

"Nothing!"

I raced to the next mirror and looked into his living room. Again there were shelves lined with books. There were paintings on the wall, but the only photograph showed Mr. McGuire standing with my grandfather in front of their original magic repair shop. There were no pictures of anyone else that would let me know who his true love might be.

The fourth mirror yielded a view of a small kitchenette. A lone cookie jar sat on the counter next to a bowl of fruit and dishes sitting in a drying rack.

I walked back to the bedroom mirror and looked again. I leaned in close and tried to read the titles of the books on the shelves. I stared at the figurines scattered among the books, and my eyes widened.

I rushed to the living room mirror and looked at the titles of the books in there, and then at the paintings hanging on the walls. "That's got to be it," I said, my heart racing. I looked in the bathroom and nodded as I took in the pattern on the shower curtain. A huge smile burst onto my face as I ran full speed from the room.

"They have the dragon," Milo had said.

Habanero was the answer!

12

It's What's on the Inside
That Counts

I ran full speed back through the mirror shard.

"Anything?" Fiona asked nervously. "We only have *two* more minutes!"

"It's Habanero!" I cried.

Habanero's head jerked up, and he trilled.

"What? The old man's in love with *the dragon*?" Hasenpfeffer said. "You can't be serious?"

I shook my head. "No! Not Habanero, but dragons in general. His house is filled with books on dragons. There are paintings of dragons on the wall and small figures on his shelves. Even his shower curtain has dragons on it!"

Darcy laughed. "Sounds more like an obsession."

"Yes," I said, "a wonderful, wonderful obsession." I pointed to the bed. "Habanero, you have to lick Mr. McGuire—on the lips."

The dragon cocked his head and looked over to Mr. McGuire. He chirped questioningly.

"Oh, just do it!" Hasenpfeffer said. "He doesn't have cooties. At least not that I'm aware of."

Habanero slowly approached the bed and sniffed Mr. McGuire.

"We're running out of time. Do it," Darcy said, "and I'll give you a nice pepper." Habanero's eyes lit up. Darcy waved her wand over her palm, and a pepper appeared. "Give the old man a kiss, and this is yours."

Habanero nodded his head and leaned over Mr. McGuire. He sniffed once more and then stuck out his long black tongue and licked Mr. McGuire across the lips. He pulled away, and steam poured from his nostrils as he shook his head with curled-up lips. Darcy tossed the pepper into the air, and the dragon caught it in his mouth and chewed happily.

Mr. McGuire's eyelids fluttered open, and then he slowly sat up in the bed. "Goodness," he said, looking around. He reached up and touched his face. "Why is my face all wet?"

I ran to the bed, threw my arms around Mr. McGuire, and buried my face on his chest. "We did it!" I sobbed.

"Maggie!" he exclaimed. "I'm—I'm awake. That means . . ." He pulled back and beamed at me. "You won! You did it! How did you know what would wake me?"

"I got help—from the kobold."

"The kobold?" Darcy and Fiona said in unison.

Suddenly the mirrors around us cracked and shattered with an earsplitting clatter. Hasenpfeffer leapt up onto the bed, and as the walls fell and disappeared, we found ourselves in the throne room.

"You helped them?" Milo roared as he pushed himself off his throne and raced down the steps with his wand raised, eyes blazing.

Hasenpfeffer dove under a pillow, and Habanero trilled nervously.

The kobold jumped up from his stool. "No! They've won fair and square," he insisted.

Milo's face was flushed with anger; he narrowed his eyes and glared at me. "Was it 'fair and square'?"

"I, um . . ."

Milo sneered. "Not that we could trust *you* to tell the truth."

I stood tall and looked Milo in the eye. "Okay, we got a little help—but not like you think."

Milo turned to the kobold, pulling on his long mustache. "I wondered how they made it through the maze so quickly, and how they could've figured out that the dragon was the way to wake McGuire. To think *I trusted* you!"

The kobold jutted his chin out. "I told them *nothing*."

"He didn't!" I said. "I was in the mirrors and overheard you talking."

"But he did *help*," Milo said, his voice dripping with venom. He turned to the kobold. "You go on and on about your fair play, but you couldn't keep from helping them." He turned and pointed a long finger at me. "Helping *her*—the girl who trapped me in mirror. The granddaughter of the man who trapped you!"

The kobold frowned and chewed on his black nails. "I—I . . ."

"Just admit it already!" Milo shouted. "You cheated; therefore, I win my freedom!"

"If he did help us," I said, "it's because he's an honorable creature, unlike you!"

"Honorable?" Milo sneered. "It was so honorable of him to kidnap your friends and trap them in the mirror?"

"I am honorable!" the kobold insisted. "And it was you who came up with the idea."

"And," Milo continued, "I'm sure you were locked up in a block of salt because you were *honorable*."

"That was all a mistake!" the kobold spat. "I was innocent, just like you."

I ran up to Milo. "Innocent?" I turned to the kobold. "He lied! I *didn't* trap him in the mirror. He was going to send me into the mirror even after I told him his duplicate was powerless! It was his own ego and selfishness that got him trapped."

Milo waved a hand dismissively in the air. "Lies, lies, and more lies. The depths to which you sink are utterly amazing."

"But she's telling the truth!" Mr. McGuire said. "I was there."

Darcy put her hands on her hips. "Me too!"

Fiona nodded as well.

The kobold looked back and forth between Milo and me. "I don't know what to believe anymore."

"There's only one way to settle this," I said. "We need to show what's inside us—what's really in our hearts."

Milo scoffed. "And how do you propose to do that?"

"With a spell." I walked toward one of the mirrors leaning against the wall. "Mr. McGuire, do you know a spell that will reflect what's inside?"

He walked up to the mirror, clucking his tongue. "When I was researching reflection spells to rescue Aitan's, I did find one that might work."

Milo threw his hands into the air. "Oh, this is ridiculous! The girl's a liar and the troll's a cheat!"

The kobold seethed. "I am *not* a troll! Trolls are twisted creatures with black hearts."

Milo pursed his lips and folded his arms across his chest. "I stand by my words."

"What is this spell, Mr. McGuire?" the kobold asked. "I need to prove to you all that I am an honorable creature who was unjustly imprisoned."

"Come to the mirrors," Mr. McGuire said. "The three of you."

Milo raised his large nose into the air and sniffed. "I have no interest in participating in your silly little spell casting."

"I will honor our bargain only if you comply," the kobold said. "If you're heart proves honorable, I will set you free, because I *did* help Maggie—even if it was just a tiny bit."

Milo nibbled on his lower lip, and then he raised his nose in the air again. "Very well. I have nothing to hide."

Mr. McGuire pushed three mirror fragments side by side, and Milo, the kobold, and I stood in front of them. "Think about what is truly in your heart," Mr. McGuire said.

I took a deep breath and stared at my reflection. My

hair was a tangled mess of knots and cobwebs, and dark soot stained my face, but I knew inside that I was right and Milo was the liar. Mr. McGuire wiped his brow and then took out his wand.

"Do you need any ingredients?" I asked.

He gently shook his head. "Not for this one."

He held his wand aloft. *"Reflection of the heart, shine bright for all to see. Reflect what's inside and set your soul free."*

I inhaled as my reflection changed. My hair was brushed and my cheeks rosy. A warm glow radiated around me, and I smiled. I turned to look at the kobold's reflection and saw a sunny glow emanating from his serene image in the glass.

The kobold gasped and pointed to the third mirror. I turned to see Milo's face looking like it had aged fifty years. An oily black mist swirled around him, and despite everything I knew about him, the hate radiating from the mirror took my breath away.

"You can't hide what's inside, and now everyone knows!" I said to Milo. I turned to the kobold. "You can't set him free. You see that, don't you?"

The kobold slowly nodded. "I—I had no idea."

Milo wrinkled his nose. "This is nothing but an illusion to trick you! They've conspired against me—conjured up this phony spell to make me look bad. Just watch. I, too, can make a bright and shiny reflection." He took his wand out and pointed it at the mirror reflecting his twisted soul. *"Call the power of the sun; use its rays to shine. From gold dust to daffodils, make it mine!"*

Milo's reflection flared up in a glittering array of gold and rainbow-colored light so bright that I had to turn away and shield my eyes.

"Ha! Look!" he commanded. "See how pure my soul is! Look at it shimmer brighter than any of yours. I am the Master of Mirrors! I have triumphed, and I demand to be set free!"

Suddenly a misty image began to form in the room. "Gregory?" Mr. McGuire gasped. "Is that you?"

A man with curly hair and a bow tie—my grandfather—materialized in front of Milo's mirror.

"I'm sorry," he whispered, looking at the kobold. *"It's time to set things right. Buhodu!"* he called.

His misty form stepped aside as a throaty bellow echoed from the mirror bearing Milo's reflection. In a flash the white crocodile appeared in the mirror and snapped its jaws at Milo's reflection. The magician gasped and his eyes went blank as Buhodu shook his head and turned, disappearing in the mirror with the sparkling reflection dangling from his mouth.

The kobold rushed toward Milo and pushed him into

the shard. He then snapped his fingers, and all of the mirrors in the room exploded.

Screams echoed around the room, and we raised our arms to shield our heads from the shattering glass. Seconds later we stood in the misty fog, the castle and the maze—everything—gone.

I stared at my friends, breathing heavily but glad to see that everyone was okay.

"Is it over?" Hasenpfeffer whimpered as he hopped over to me.

Mr. McGuire gestured to the kobold, who nodded his head.

"Yes, and I'm sorry for all I put you through," the creature said. "Maggie, I'm sorry I misjudged you, as I was misjudged before."

My grandfather's ghost bowed his head. *"I can't take back what I did; I can only hope you can forgive me."*

The kobold nodded. "I do, and I ask that you can forgive me for what I put your granddaughter through."

Grandpa Malloy turned to me. *"Maggie, my time here is brief. Already I feel the tug of sleep beckoning me, but I want you to know that I'm proud of you. I wish your father and I had used our magic for good, as you have. You have a powerful gift. Please remember to use it wisely."*

The kobold cleared his throat. "Before you go,

Mr. Malloy, I want to let you know. . . . I wouldn't have let anyone come to any harm. The flames in Hansel and Gretel's house would not have burnt the rabbit. The spiders—they carried no venom. And, well . . ." He turned to me. "I made sure you found out about the dragon," he said with a wink.

Darcy and I exchanged looks. "We went through all of that for *nothing*?" Darcy griped.

"No," the kobold said, "not for nothing. It's true that when I first met Milo I was filled with hatred and thoughts of revenge, but I couldn't shake the feeling that my anger was misdirected—that Maggie shouldn't have to pay for what her grandfather had done to me. And I was not happy carrying all that anger. I couldn't let the blackness destroy my soul—like it did Milo's. I couldn't destroy the contract—it's bound by powerful fairy magic—but I made sure no one would get hurt."

Darcy scowled. "But someone did!"

The kobold shook his head. "Look behind you."

Darcy turned, and coming through the mist was Marilla. Darcy ran to her and threw her arms around the giant mantis's neck.

"Excuse me, but do you have a name?" Fiona asked.

The kobold looked up, surprised. "You want to know *my* name?"

"Yes. I want to know who to thank for helping us."

The kobold smiled and gave a slight bow. "My name is Forest."

I walked over to Fiona and the kobold. "Thank you, Forest," I said.

"Yes, thank you," Fiona echoed.

He grinned. "You're welcome." Tears glistened in Forest's eyes. "I only wanted to help your father. That is what kobolds wish to do—to help—to be useful. But Michael had so much anger in him."

I knelt down and took Forest's hand in mine. "I'm sorry about what happened to you, and I know I can't make it right, but you're *free* now."

Forest hung his head. "But I don't want to be free," he said. "I long only to serve."

"Maybe we can—" I gasped. "Oh, no. They're going to recreate the capture spell—only this time it's permanent.

I pulled the compact out of my pocket and opened it. "Maggie!" Raphael said with a huge grin. "We're almost done. One minute and counting, and then it's 'Good-bye, kobold!'"

"No!" I yelled. "Don't do it! You have to stop them! Forest—*the kobold*—he's on our side. He never should have been trapped in the first place. *Stop them!*"

Raphael dropped the compact, and shouting ensued. I took Forest's hand in mine again and held my breath.

His eyes widened and he started to fade. "You did your best," he said quietly. "After what I put you through, I deserve it."

"No! Raphael, stop them! Please!"

Forest looked up at me, a tear in his eye. "It's okay. The world has changed. There's no place for a creature such as myself. . . ."

I grabbed at Forest's fading hand. *"I wish the spell wouldn't work! I wish Forest remains just as he is!"*

"No!" My grandfather shrieked as he saw Forest fade even more. *"I won't let this happen again!"* He dissolved into a misty haze and rushed into the compact.

I bit my lip and hoped we weren't too late.

13

Ever After

The next day Raphael, Fiona, Darcy, and I headed down to the repair shop after we'd finished working on our puppet shows for Ms. Wiggins. As we jogged down the stairs, we could hear shouting. We rushed in to see Mrs. Davenport arguing with Mr. McGuire.

"I don't care how *attached* Darcy is to that—that *thing*. I want you to come over and get it out of my house!"

"Mother!" Darcy said. "I told you, Marilla is staying."

Mrs. Davenport pointed a finger in Mr. McGuire's face. "This is all your fault! If you hadn't had that infernal mirror, Darcy never would've gotten sucked in, and she never would've come home with that giant *beetle!*"

Raphael, Fiona, and I exchanged amused looks as Mr. McGuire nervously played with his suspenders. Forest was peeking through the back curtains, and a smile broke out on my face. My wish magic, with help from my grandfather, had spared Forest—and created a tremendous rainstorm that had melted the salt they'd been using to encase the poppet. When we'd finally stepped out of the mirror last night, there'd been a lot of wet—and happy—people in the shop.

Well, except Gram. I know she wished she could have spoken to Grandpa Malloy for longer, but once Forest was safe, Grandpa Malloy was called back to wherever it was he came from. I think Gram was happy to know the truth about the kobold, but I also knew it would take her a long time to make peace with what had happened to my father and her husband.

"It's a *mantis*, Mother," Darcy said. "Not a beetle."

Mrs. Davenport waved a hand in the air. "I don't care what it is! It's repulsive, and Muffin Cakes, my shih tzu, refuses to come out from under the bed."

"Well, Daddy and Gammy Davenport like her."

"What if you downsize it a bit?" Mr. McGuire asked. "I have some shrinking powder I could give you—free of charge."

Mrs. Davenport sniffed. "Fine! Give me the powder, and I'll be on my way. Are you finished with your little project?" she asked Darcy.

Darcy nodded, and Mrs. Davenport rolled her eyes. "We're trying to prepare her for Harvard, and Ms. Wiggins is assigning *puppet shows*," she muttered.

Mr. McGuire poured what looked like green sand into a small jar and then put the jar into a paper bag. "Here you are," he said, handing it to Mrs. Davenport. "Every teaspoon will shrink exactly one foot off her size. You can decide how small you'd like her to get."

She snatched the bag from him and wrinkled her nose at the magic mirror in the corner of the shop. "It's a good thing you're voluntarily getting rid of that mirror, or I would've gone straight to Sir Lachlan to have it forcibly removed! I will see that Viola Klemp mounts a full investigation to see if this whole debacle could've been avoided. Come, Darcy!"

I waved. "I'll see you in school on Monday. I think Ms. Wiggins will love our show."

Darcy grinned. We'd created shadow puppets, with a little magical help. The hearts we'd cut out would glow like "blossoming stars." "We're going to kick butt! Maximilian Litmann is going down!" she said.

"Darcy!" her mother admonished. "Watch your

language!" She shook her head and looked over her shoulder at me. "Looks like someone is a bad influence." She stuck her nose into the air and then marched to the door.

"Bye!" Raphael and Fiona said.

When the door shut, Forest came through the curtains. "Milo's cousin, eh? I see the family resemblance."

"At least Darcy's come around," I said. "She even invited us to her birthday party!"

"I think we're all a good influence on her," Raphael said. "If you ask me, the less time Darcy spends with her mother the better."

I looked up at the clock hanging behind the counter. "Forest, Mr. Webb will be here any minute."

Forest looked down, straightened his shirt, and ran his clawed fingers through his messy hair. "Do I look all right?"

Fiona smiled. "Perfect!"

The front door cracked opened, and Mr. Webb poked his head in. "Is the coast clear?" he asked.

"All clear," Mr. McGuire said.

Mr. Webb opened the door all the way, and the five house brownies scuttled in, their wide eyes staring at Forest. Mr. Webb walked over to Forest and bent over to shake his hand. "Are you the fellow interested in joining the troop and performing with the Webb Family's Stringless Marionettes?"

Forest grinned and nodded. "Oh, before my old family brought me to America, we used to read *Grimm's Fairy Tales* all the time. When Maggie told me about your puppet show, it sounded like a dream come true! I've been idle so long, it will be great to have a purpose once again."

Mr. Webb beamed. "Do you hear that, you ungrateful brownies? Here's someone who's looking forward to working!"

"He hasn't read the script yet," one of them muttered.

Mr. Webb frowned, but Forest perked up even more. "Oh, may I?" he asked.

The brownies exchanged knowing looks. "Show him the script," another said.

"It's not perfect," Mr. Webb said. "There have been some complaints." He eyed the brownies for a second and then gave Forest a copy of the script to *Hansel and Gretel*. Forest jumped up onto the stool behind the counter and opened it up.

"It *is* pretty bad," Raphael whispered.

Fiona glared at him. "Shh!"

Forest began shaking his head. "Oh, this definitely needs a rewrite." He looked over the counter at the house brownies, who were all nodding in agreement. "I can see why you were having trouble performing the show. The dialogue is . . . "

Forest looked sheepishly at Mr. Webb. "No offense. I'm sure you did your best.

But as an avid reader of fairy tales, I'm confident I can spruce up this script to everyone's satisfaction."

Mr. Webb walked up to the counter. "There's only one thing I'll be needing, then."

Forest smiled, reached below the counter, and came up with his wooden poppet. He gave it to Mr. Webb and smiled. "I have a new family?"

"You have a new family," Mr. Webb said. "Come, there is much work to be done before our next show."

As Mr. Webb said his good-byes to Mr. McGuire, I drew Forest aside. "Do you think my father—Do you think he would've ended up like Milo if he hadn't lost his magic?"

Forest looked away. "No, of course not. He was just a bit . . . rambunctious."

I sighed. "Thanks for trying to spare my feelings."

"No, he . . . he could've changed. We'll never know, though, and maybe that's for the best," Forest whispered.

He held out his hand, and I took it in mine, marveling how just yesterday the sight of it on my bedroom door had filled me with fear. "Thank you for believing in me," I whispered.

He touched his heart. "And thank you for believing in *me*," he said.

"Puppets, let's move out," Mr. Webb shouted. "We have to be in Pittsburgh tomorrow, and there's so much to do."

Just as Mr. Webb was rounding up his brownies, the door slammed open and Viola Klemp stormed in, followed by three other women.

Viola regarded the brownies and shook her head. "Mr. Webb!" she said sharply. "Is there a reason you've got brownies out and about where the general public can see them?"

Mr. Webb gulped, and Fiona and I shared a nervous look. We knew Viola would want to get her hands on Forest, so we had told her that he was still in the mirror. Forest shuffled his way toward the brownies, and they surrounded him so that he looked like one of their own.

"Now, Viola," Mr. Webb said. "There's no one out and about here on this deserted street, and the van is parked right at the top of the stairs."

Viola looked down her large hooked nose at Mr. Webb. "Nevertheless, I shall be forced to issue you a warning. Expect it in the mail!"

Mr. Webb's shoulders slumped. "Can't wait."

He opened the door, and the brownies and Forest raced up the stairs.

"Now," Viola said. "We're ready for the mirror."

The three women with Viola gathered in front of it, whispering and reaching out to touch the blue cover. They were all dressed in dark gray pantsuits, and they all shared Viola's sharp features.

"What do you have planned for it?" Mr. McGuire asked. He looked at the mirror with a wrinkled brow. I knew how much he had treasured it—before Milo had arrived. And I also knew he was ready to give it away.

Viola narrowed her eyes. "We're going to study it in a controlled environment. While Milo is likely . . . dead"—she glanced at me—"we can't rule out the possibility that he may have survived the crocodile attack. And there is the kobold. I may be back to get more testimony from the children about what went on inside the mirror before we wrap up our investigation into yesterday's events, but we can't just take the word of *children* that the kobold is not a creature that needs to be dragged out of the mirror and prosecuted to the fullest powers of the Society of Ethical Magicians."

Mr. McGuire nodded and turned away, avoiding eye contact with Viola.

"Maggie," Viola said.

I looked up with reddening cheeks.

"A lot of things—*bad things*—have happened since you arrived in Bridgeport. You've brought non-magical people into our world." She glared at Raphael and Fiona. "We'll be watching you. I suggest you keep your nose clean. The society is planning on making some big changes—changes you don't want to be on the wrong side of."

She strutted over to the mirror. "Are we ready, ladies?"

The women opened their purses and took out matching trim, compact wands. They murmured a spell, and the mirror rose a foot from the floor. Holding their wands out, they levitated the mirror to the door. A hawkish woman with short gray curls opened it and peeked outside. She turned back. "We're good," she said, and they floated the mirror out of the shop and slammed the door shut.

I exhaled. The second the door shut, I felt like a great weight was lifted from my shoulders. "Things are going to be okay now, aren't they?"

Mr. McGuire nodded. "I think so."

I heard a trill, and then a pint-size Habanero stretched out his neck and yawned from the spot where he'd been sleeping on top of the bookshelves. Mr. McGuire beamed at the dragon as he put the shrinking powder back onto the shelf. "Who's hungry?" he cooed to the foot-long dragon.

Habanero licked his lips, and Mr. McGuire tossed a small chili pepper into the air. Habanero swooped up and caught it, making Mr. McGuire laugh like a boy with his dog. "Never did I imagine I'd have a dragon," he said. "Some good came of yesterday's awful events, and more good is to follow. I can feel it in my bones."

I nodded and looked around the shop.

But when dealing with magic, I'd learned to expect the unexpected.

Rachel Renée Russell

DORK diaries

The *New York Times* Bestselling Series

Tales from a NOT-SO- Popular Party Girl

Recipe for disaster:

4 parties. Add 2 friends and 1 crush. Divide by 1 mean girl out to ruin Nikki. Mix well, put fingers over eyes, and cringe!

From Aladdin
Published by Simon & Schuster

Goddess Girls

READ ABOUT ALL YOUR FAVORITE GODDESSES!

#1 ATHENA THE BRAIN

#2 PERSEPHONE THE PHONY

#3 APHRODITE THE BEAUTY

#4 ARTEMIS THE BRAVE

From Aladdin

PUBLISHED BY SIMON & SCHUSTER

GET READY TO LAUGH OUT LOUD WITH THESE HILARIOUS BOOKS FROM ALADDIN!